A STRANGER AT THE HEARTH

A STRANGER AT THE HEARTH

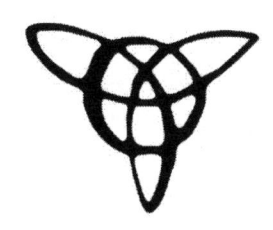

THE NORSE SAGA OF SIGURD

KATHERINE BUEL

This is a work of fiction. All of the characters, organizations, and events are either products of the author's imagination or are used fictitiously.

A STRANGER AT THE HEARTH. Copyright © 2022 by Katherine Buel. All rights reserved.

No part of this publication may be reproduced, distributed, or transmitted in any form or by any means, including photocopying, recording, or other electronic or mechanical methods, without the prior written permission of the publisher, except in the case of brief quotations for review purposes.

ISBN-13: 9798838037893

Also by Katherine Buel

THE NORSE SAGA OF SIGURD
A Stranger at the Hearth
The Roots of Yggdrasil

THE GRIEVER'S MARK
The Griever's Mark
Chains of Water and Stone
Unbound

FAERIE TALES RICH & STRANGE
White as Witching

*Dark grows the sun, and in summer soon
Come mighty storms: would you know yet more?*

—"THE WISE WOMAN'S PROPHECY,"
THE POETIC EDDA, TRANSLATED
BY HENRY ADAMS BELLOWS, 1923

Prologue

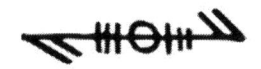

SCATTERED SWORDS AND BROKEN spears winked back the first bloody light of dawn. Carrion birds wheeled over the battlefield. Noisy on their wings, they were neither so furtive nor so shameful in their thieving as the men who crept among the dead, pilfering blades and rings. Wolves stalked the edges of the field, dragging away what they might.

Where night's shade yet lingered along the forest border, the young queen, belly round and firm beneath her blue woolen dress, knelt beside grey-bearded King Sigmund. She had found him before the dew rose from the ground, when he could still speak. He had been angry with her then, because she should have fled, to save herself and their unborn son from the invaders. After all, it was for her they had come in their dragonships. But Hjordis would not leave the king.

He was red to the shoulders with the blood of his enemies, yet Odin's will had turned from him at last. The god himself had joined the battle and shattered the king's sword, that very sword he himself had once given to Sigmund—now lost. When the blade had burst, Sigmund's men had begun to fall fast around him, but he did not turn from his fate. On he fought, fey and reckless, in the way of a bright, doomed warrior. But as skalds sing to the tune of their six-stringed harps: *No might against many.* Sigmund fell at last.

Now, with the blood of his death-wound crusting his broken byrnie, his eyes stared, sightless, into the paling sky. Hjordis kissed Sigmund's cold lips and pressed her warm cheek against his waxen one. Then she raised her head, her fine, pale hair catching on the mail rings. Odin stood behind her. He had been there for some time, one-eyed and grim, his white braids hanging to his belt and his spear terrible beside him.

"You must go now," Odin said when Hjordis had drawn a hand over Sigmund's unseeing eyes. "Lygni has already discovered you absent from the hall."

Wearied beyond courtesy, the young queen did not even look at the god. "And just where do you expect me to go?"

"Another fleet is landing on the coast. Ælf, son of King Hjalprek of Denmark, leads them. Your future lies there."

When Hjordis had chosen Sigmund over Lygni, she had joined herself to an uncertainty—she had known that. Four years ago, on the first night of his visit to her father, Sigmund had sat by the hearth fire and told the tale demanded of him: how he had pulled Odin's sword from the Branstock's great trunk when no other could shift it. She had known then that he was dangerous. Not because he was descended from Odin, nor because of the godly sword, but because his expression as he spoke—eerie, unfocused—was not quite human. Her father's kingdom was small and quiet, and she had wanted to be part of something greater, had known herself to be strong enough. But she had not understood, then, what it would mean to be woven into someone else's pattern, caught up in someone else's fate.

"You're not here for me. You're here for my son. It is his future you are shaping, not mine." She spoke with certainty and a little bitterness.

From the shadow of his wide-brimmed hat, Odin gazed down at her with his lone eye and warned, "Don't meddle with me, woman."

"Maybe I will wait and wed my enemy, as many women have done before. Maybe I will find my vengeance in poison and fire, as many women have done before."

"And waste your son in the doing?"

Fear chilled Hjordis's blood, and she laid a hand over the mound of her belly. Once, she had thrilled at tales of grand and vengeful women. She had thought herself to burn as bright. But she knew in an instant that she would not risk her child. So quickly was she made a mother, and nothing else.

"And who will avenge my husband? Who will balance this, Betrayer of Warriors? Not you."

Odin was growing impatient. "Cease your foolish questions and save your son. You know how it must be."

"How it must be, Allfather—or how you will it?"

But Odin was done with her, for he knew he had won and that her words were only her own heartache, and no concern of his. He vanished between one blink and the next.

Cursing her lot, Hjordis with her handmaiden went down to the shore, where Ælf's men were securing their ships. Gleaming in his clean, unblemished armor, Ælf crossed the beach to meet the women. He was handsome and charming; he was young, as Sigmund had not been. He had thick, beautiful hair, and he smiled at Hjordis, his teeth white and even. She was unimpressed.

When she identified herself, Ælf offered her sanctuary, but he wanted to know what had become of Sigmund's wealth, for the fame of his treasure hoard was widespread. Hjordis then looked on him with some respect—at least he wasn't a complete fool—and she took him to the cave where Sigmund had hidden that treasure from Lygni's invading army. If she left the gold, Lygni's men might someday find it, and so it would go instead to Denmark with her and Ælf and Sigmund's unborn son.

After a long travail, Hjordis bore her son in a foreign land. She strained and wept and lay back weary on the bed, and finally she held the babe to her breast. The women, all strangers but for her maid, Asta, gathered around. They smiled at the babe and at the mother, who would soon marry Ælf and would one day be their queen. But the child was strange, too quiet, his eyes too keen for one so newly born. The women muttered and glanced at one another. Hjordis cast them a scornful look that sent them scraping from the room.

Her son was beautiful. She wondered if he would look like his father and how she would know if he did, for Sigmund had been well past his sixtieth winter when they married. Sigmund, who had so often been distant, had smiled wonderfully when he learned he would have another son; all his others, all his kin, were dead. Alone now as she had never been, Hjordis thought she knew what he must have felt, that this child would connect him again to the world.

Deep in her mind, she knew he was not truly hers. Odin would claim him. The Norns, spinning and weaving men's fates at the base of the world-tree, would claim him. Even now, shadows moved through the room, dancing away from the hearth fire's flickering light, skittering along the tapestry-hung walls, coiling even around the bed's raven-carved posts. Spirits, she knew, drawn to the new life, wise to the child's fate—but silent. Another mother might have pleaded with them, begged for words, or kindness. But Hjordis would not waste this single precious moment when the babe was hers alone, for it would not last.

Whispering in the bloodstained bed, she told her son of his kin the Volsungs. All their glory and suffering she related, that of Odin's son Sigi and his son Rerir, also of Volsung, mighty father of Sigmund, and of Sigmund himself. She told the babe, too, how his father had had a deep laugh, though few ever heard it, how he had touched her round, delicate belly so gently with his warrior's hands. It was the last time she spoke thus of Sigmund. Later her son would ask about his father, wanting to know such things as she told him now. But she would turn cold at these questions. She would turn away from his hurt expression, her brief life with Sigmund buried within her. But as she lay with her son small and soft against her breast, she did speak of his father, and the sweet pain of those memories overwhelmed her.

When Asta heard Hjordis weeping, she shook off the spell of the child, whose otherness had unsettled even her. She went to the bedside. "This is all nonsense," she said, pressing a damp cloth to her lady's face. "Those fools started it. It's only natural you should feel overcome, what with all that's happened."

"My sensible Asta. Thank the gods you've come with me."

When Hjordis was sleeping, Asta took the babe to the Mead Hall, where she would find King Hjalprek. With the boy's father dead, the naming was the king's duty. Surrounded by his loyal, war-hardened thanes, Hjalprek sat in his great carved chair by the hearth fire, a gold-banded mead horn in hand. The plucked notes of a skald's harp drifted among the men's low speech.

Gold rings flashing on his arm, Hjalprek raised a hand for silence. Then it could be heard: ravens cawing, their sharp voices piercing down through the smoke vents in the hall's high roof as they circled above. This too: somewhere in the distant woods, wolves howled. Folk of the north knew well these omens. The creatures that feast on the dead were rejoicing, for a warrior had been born.

The men looked to the back of the hall, where Asta had emerged with the silent babe. She pinched the boy's leg. He began to wail then, and the king grinned through his dark beard.

"Listen to that, Ælf," he said to his son. "Lungs like a smith's bellows."

As Ælf watched Asta hand Hjalprek the child, he stood to the side, awkward, unsure whether this moment had made of him father, brother—or nothing at all. Hjalprek, on the other hand, looked wholly at ease, like a man holding his own infant son. Seeing that, Ælf knew with painful certainty that it was hope and anticipation in his father's face.

Hjalprek considered the babe as it curled a tiny hand around his calloused finger. "Look at that grip! Nearly ready for a sword! But then—he is a Volsung. I never thought to greet such a man in my hall, yet now I am holding one in my arms, imagining what he will become." Then he declared, "I name him Sigurd, Warder of Victory," and he dipped his fingers into his mead horn and sprinkled the babe. Sigurd made a face but did not cry, staring back at Hjalprek in his strange way.

"Yes," marveled the king, his eyes bright with joy, "Warder of Victory."

Chapter One

WHEN SIGURD WAS NEARING fourteen winters of age, Hjalprek was brought home from battle with a wound in his thigh and it festered. He lay for many days in his chamber. Sigurd, hand clumsy with bandages, for two of his fingers had been broken in the fighting, held a cup to the king's lips.

"I wish you would go," Hjalprek grumbled as Sigurd wiped a spill from his chin. "It's bad enough without you playing nursemaid."

Sigurd scowled at the king. "You might get better, you know, if you would try."

Hjalprek's face, once so ruddy, had grown as grey as the streaks in his beard, and his eyes were dull. Despite the herbs burning in the brazier, the room stank of corrupted flesh.

"Someday, boy, when death is sitting on your chest, you will know your body be no more use to you. I only hope you'll die on the field, not sweating out your strength into the straw of your pallet."

It was the fear of any warrior: to die a straw-death and thus displease the valkyries, for it was from the blood and muck of the battlefield that those bright shield-maidens chose the glorious dead for Odin's honored hall of Valhalla. But Hjalprek's life-thread had spun out a few days too long.

Sigurd left his stool and went to throw more wood on the fire, making the flames burst. "The valkyries will know your death is a battle-death. They will not fault you."

The boy's certainty almost teased a smile from the king's pain-hardened face. Age brought with it so many doubts.

Knowing the sight would soon be gone from him, Hjalprek watched Sigurd standing before the brazier with his arms crossed. Muscled from his sword-work and hunting, the boy was already growing into a man's form. His face was losing its youthful roundness, the strong bones of jaw and cheek taking shape. His hair shone like waves of gold, brilliant in the light from the window, gleaming like the sun on the sea. At his side hung the sword Hjalprek had given him. The pattern-welded blade had been Hjalprek's own as a youth.

During the battle, Sigurd's first, when they pushed the Northern Jutes once again beyond the fjord, Hjalprek had watched the boy plunge that sword into a man's throat. Most boys, even those who eventually made fighting men, stumbled into their first kill. Sigurd had leaped.

Hjalprek's rasping breath brought Sigurd back to grip the cold, knotted fingers lying on the woolen blanket. The king strained up from death's grip for a moment to throw a few final words into the world. "Be wary, boy, my arm is no longer around you."

The women tended the king's body while his son and thanes hauled his ship onto the riverbank and propped it up on timbers. A tent was raised on the deck, a bed placed inside, and all things were made ready for the king's journey. New clothes were sewn and two feasts prepared—one for the living, one for the dead—and the concubine who had shared the king's bed since his wife's death was chosen to travel with him.

During these days of preparation, many men came to Hjalprek's stronghold. He was a far-known king, his wealth and warring much respected. At night, the raised platforms running the length of the king's hall, all paneled with smooth oak and hung with antlers, were more crowded than usual with mead-drunk men. On the eve of the burning, while most yet lingered around the great hearth fires, one last guest came into the hall.

Sigurd, sitting with Ælf and the king's thanes, was at this time listening to a skald sing of the clash between fire and ice that birthed the first evil of the world: the giant, Ymir. Sigurd shivered at the song, as all must, for endless years of battle raged through the primordial vastness before Odin and his brothers slew Ymir and hacked him into pieces and from his shattered flesh fashioned the world of men. Of his bones they made the mountains, of his blood was born the world's waters, and from the vault of his skull did the gods shape the sky.

The skald broke off, harp notes fading, leaving the world half formed as the guards guided the late-come guest to the hearth. Though Ælf's pale skin was flushed with drink, when he stood from his father's carven chair, he looked suddenly quite sober.

Sigurd noted how the gathered men stiffened and glanced at one another, and he gave the stranger a guarded look. His hair was dark even to blackness and he wore plain, dark clothes with no silver flashing upon them, nor any rings did he display on his arms. Despite this, he walked with a self-possession that a king might envy. His mouth was set in a firm, unforgiving line. As he neared the hearth, his high cheekbones caught the fire's glow, casting shadows up his face. Sigurd heard someone mutter, "Master of Masters," and a shudder passed through him.

"Hail, Regin," Ælf greeted the man. "I didn't expect you for another week at least. You must have killed three horses to get here so fast."

The man called Regin replied, "How could I miss your father's funeral, when he was a son to me?"

Ælf frowned. "A foster son, yes. He always respected your skill and ... wisdom."

Regin had eerily pale eyes that glittered like ice in the firelight, and those eyes drifted to Sigurd. "The Volsung boy?"

Ælf impatiently motioned Sigurd to stand. "Sigurd, son of Sigmund, son of Volsung. My ward."

If Regin marked this designation—not son, nor even stepson, but ward—he made no sign of it. He focused on the boy, drawing in his chin thoughtfully as he gazed upon a bruised cheek, the splinted fingers. "What happened to your hand, boy?"

"Just some fingers broken in a skirmish," said Ælf before Sigurd could answer.

Sigurd made a face, not liking to be spoken for. He quickly smoothed the rudeness from his expression, but Regin had seen—and seemed to delight in it. "He's bold enough to speak for himself, I think. Come, boy, did you kill the man who trod on your fingers?"

Sigurd answered, "Someone put a spear in his back before I had the chance. But he didn't tread on my fingers. He broke my shield."

"Broke your shield, did he?" echoed Regin, a hint of mockery in his tone.

"It won't happen again," Sigurd declared.

"Oh? And why is that?"

"Because the only thing between me and my enemies will be my sword, not my shield." He would not again hide behind a circle of wood. He hated how frightened he had been in that moment, bracing for pain or death. Better, he had decided, to attack, better to feel the power of action.

Pale eyes narrowing, Regin seemed to weigh this answer. Then he laughed, low and with a peculiar joy. "He is a Volsung, isn't he? So wonderfully impractical. Whatever will you do with him, Ælf?"

"He's a child yet. There is time to decide," Ælf answered stiffly then motioned the men on the bench to make room. "You must be hungry, Regin. Have some meat and tell us the news from the south."

As more meat was eaten and more mead drunk, the conversation turned to battles and plunder, to the weather and the harvest. Regin spoke little, holding back. No one pressed him. Sigurd listened for a time, but the talk was familiar and dull. Quietly he left the hearth and wound his way around the tables and men. As he reached the passageway to the private chambers, his scalp prickled in a way that made him look back. Regin, from his place at the hearth, was watching him.

Sigurd found his mother with her women, finishing the embroidery on the king's tunic by the light of her brazier and several smoking candles. With the funeral shirt puddled in her lap, his mother's quick hands sent the needle dipping in and out of the blue linen, appearing and disappearing like a ship in a swell. Without halting her work, Hjordis lifted her eyes to Sigurd in the doorway, then she sent her women, even Asta, from the room. When they were gone, Sigurd came to sit in the golden rushes at her feet.

Hjordis continued her needlework. Time had taught her endurance and separateness, and she liked her son's silent ways. Even when he had been learning to speak, she had never pressed him into childish conversation, had never encouraged the meaningless chatter that was the delight of most mothers.

Hjordis had nearly finished the wolf's head she was working before Sigurd spoke. "There's a man here, a strange man. He came for the funeral."

Hjordis set another stitch. "Does this man have a name?"

"Ælf called him Regin."

Hjordis paused, her thread pulled halfway through the cloth. "You're certain?"

"Of course. Who is he? Everyone seemed wary of him."

"He was King Hjalprek's foster father."

Sigurd frowned and drew up his knees. "That's what Ælf said, but it doesn't make sense. This man is younger than Hjalprek."

"Oh, no—Regin is old, terribly old, too old to account for." Hjordis's hands dropped into the puddle of cloth. "They say he lived here once, generations ago, that he was the king's smith. They say his skill is beyond compare, even unnatural."

"Unnatural?"

Sigurd looked intrigued, and Hjordis chided herself for gossiping like an idle woman. She had said too much and so must say more, to warn her son. "They say he's a wizard and that he has a heart of iron and a mind as ruthless as winter. He is not to be trusted." She picked up her embroidery and began to put sails on a ship. "Did you speak with him?"

"Yes. I was not afraid."

Hjordis frowned at the funeral shirt. "Go to bed, Sigurd. Tomorrow will be a long day."

Sigurd stood in the crowd near the shore as the corpse was carried to the ship. Ælf and three of the king's thanes took the body, stiff and stinking despite the herbs sewn into the tunic, inside the tent and laid him in the bed. His dog was killed then his two best horses and two cows, horns gilded, that they might enrich him in Valhalla. Then the provisions were loaded: mead and meat, bread, fruit and leeks, also the king's weapons and treasures. Last was the king's concubine, dazed and stumbling.

Ælf took a burning branch from the fire on the shore. He walked backwards toward the ship and thrust the flaming brand into the kindling and timbers beneath. Then everyone took up fire and threw it on the wood. Soon the flames swallowed the ship. Later, when the fire had burned itself out, a mound was built and the king's ashes placed inside.

The feasting lasted many days, and a great deal of the king's wealth was spent in honoring him. The youths and men danced the battle-dance each night in the hall, leaping among the upturned spears with their weapons in hand, howling and beating their shields, remembering the king and the gods. Sigurd loved the battle-dance. He would not be as tall and broad as his father, but his build promised strength and speed and greater agility, and he could already leap higher than boys of several more winters. The men praised him at these dances, and it pleased him to be set above the others, though some loneliness came of this.

On a fine autumn day, when the funeral feasts were over, Ælf was made king in a formal ceremony within the town's temple, a large wooden building alongside the king's hall. Crowded near the entrance and stretching along the road, townsfolk and farmers waited for the new-made king to emerge.

Within, Hjalprek's kin and thanes, the distinguished guests, and high-ranking servants stood shoulder to shoulder. The temple reeked of stale sacrifice. The clay floor and paneled walls, the carved columns that were the gods in that place, even the ceiling—all were stained brown with layer upon layer of consecrated blood. Set apart from the rows of wooden gods was the column of Odin. He stood behind the stone altar, his crudely carved eye enormous and watching. His ravens gripped his shoulders; his hand gripped his spear. Upon the altar waited the blood-bowl, the blood-twig, and the knife of sacrifice. There also lay the oath-binder, the heavy gold arm-ring that the king wore in the presence of the wooden gods.

Sigurd stood between his mother and Regin as Ælf swore his oath of kingship and called on the gods to bless his rule. Then the dead king's thanes swore fealty to him on the arm-ring.

"Changes in kingship," Regin whispered to Sigurd as the speeches dragged on, "are always interesting. Once these men were Hjalprek's. Now they are Ælf's."

"Of course," said Sigurd, ignoring his mother's silencing look. "Why shouldn't they pledge themselves to Ælf?" It was the way of things. The ache in Sigurd's chest at the sight of Ælf taking Hjalprek's place mattered not at all.

"Oh, they should, of course. But wait and see. Things will be different now. These men will be different." He added, seeming to weight each word, "They will be Ælf's men."

Regin then returned his attention to the oath-giving, either unaware or uncaring that Sigurd yet regarded him. Despite what Hjordis had said of Regin, he looked nothing like a wizard—at least not as Sigurd would imagine one—and it was hard to think of him as old. Yet ... there was something about him that caught the eye, that lifted the hair on the back of the neck.

Perhaps it was just his eyes, pale and too sharp under the dark brows. But, no, Sigurd thought. It was more than that. He got a weird feeling in his stomach every time he saw Regin in the hall, sipping his mead and listening to the men, every time he spotted Regin at the edge of the training yard, watching.

The shifting of the crowd brought Sigurd's attention back to the ceremony. People were moving to make way for the animals of sacrifice, a fine young bull and three milk-fat lambs. Later, skinned and gutted, these would be impaled on spits to swell the feast.

Ælf took the knife and bowl from the altar and performed his first act as king. As he tore open each throat with the altar blade, he caught the death-blood in the bowl. Ælf dipped the blood-twig then tapped it to his forehead. The blood ran through his eyebrows, dripping onto his cheeks.

Then he moved about the temple, flicking the blood of sacrifice onto the faces of the gods, onto his thanes and the gathered men and women. Some blinked or flinched. When the warm blood splattered Sigurd's face, he held himself still. After Ælf flicked the last of the blood onto Odin's slick and shining face, the crowd hailed him as king. He returned the tools of worship and the arm-ring to the altar and led his people out of the temple, where the waiting crowd broke into cheers.

Sigurd walked behind Ælf and Hjordis, surrounded by the thanes who had sworn their new fealty. As they made their way to the hall and the feast, his thoughts returned to Regin and what he had said. In truth, Regin had not said much, but there had been a warning and a knowing in his voice—much like Hjalprek's last words.

Chapter Two

AFTER THE KING-MAKING celebration, preparations for winter resumed. Farmers and herdsmen brought the sheep, goats, and cattle in from the summer pastures, shutting the sturdy into byres for wintering, slaughtering the rest. Within the stronghold and without, women were busy with butter- and cheesemaking, and with drying fish and meat.

Early one morning, the king's hunting party assembled in the courtyard. The Mead Hall reared above them, the porch's stone steps and carved columns lost in the predawn dimness. The horses stamped and sidled, and the scent hounds shivered with excitement. The men laughed, boasting of past hunts, while those boys permitted to ride along chattered in anticipation. Even Sigurd grinned as his horse chewed impatiently at the bit. The only rider who showed no interest in the coming hunt was Regin, though none dared question his unexpected presence.

As they rode through the town, talk abated, for the four main roads, each leading to the king's hall at the center, were paved with wooden planks, and the thudding of hooves rang out like thunder from Thor's hammer. The clamor drew folk to their doorways. The houses' bowed-out sides recalled the olden days of sheltering in overturned ships, but the roofs' fine wooden shingles spoke of prosperity and security.

Indeed, the stronghold was highly defensible, with an inner and outer rampart, both built of spear-like pales, the outer one set atop a raised earthen base. As the hunting party filed through the gateway of the inner rampart, the guards stood sharp as the new king passed by them. The outer gateway tunneled through the earthen base of the rampart, and here the horses' hooves struck out a jarring echo.

As they turned off the road into the king's forest, the sun was climbing, though the grey of dawn lingered under the trees. Noses down, the scent hounds hurried through the underbrush in search of game.

Riding beside Sigurd was the grey-bearded warrior Halvar, King Hjalprek's closest friend, looking out for the boy as Hjalprek had bid him do. It was hard for Halvar—to care but not care, necessary, too, for a man whose sons were dead.

Behind Sigurd rode Jari, one of the youngest thanes, who had a patchy red beard and a large nose that inspired many jokes, mostly from Jari himself. He urged his horse up beside Sigurd's. "What possessed you to bring that doddering old pony on a hunt?"

Sigurd's bay stallion had once belonged to King Hjalprek and had been quite a fine warhorse, tall and gleaming and bearing the king with pride. Even at twenty, Gladung was powerful and handsome in his green saddle blanket and silver fittings.

"My 'doddering old pony,'" replied Sigurd, "is a true friend. Your fat little gelding would dump you in a ditch to snatch a mouthful of grass."

Jari threw back his head and laughed. "And here I thought you too spare with words to attempt the fine art of flyting. I should have known: I need only insult your horse."

"I merely speak the truth, and flyting is a stupid tradition." Better, Sigurd thought, to prove oneself rather than exchange foolish insults before a fight, as men sometimes did in a ritual flyting.

Jari struck a gloved fist to his chest. "Sigurd, you wound me. Flyting is my favorite tradition."

"Aye, it would be," observed Sigurd. "A favorite, too, of Loki's—your inspiration."

Jari directed his grin at Halvar. "His humor is turning dry already. Can you imagine him at eighteen? He'll be as shriveled as an old woman. And, Sigurd," he said quickly, not leaving room for argument, "Loki, you might remember, through his tricks and cleverness, has brought about many wonders. Since you're so fond of horses, kindly do recall how Odin's most fabulous, eight-legged steed, Sleipnir, came to be born? What's that?" Jari cupped a hand behind his ear. "Oh, yes. When a giant offered to rebuild the war-shattered wall of Asgard in exchange for not only the hand of lovely Freya but also the sun and the moon … the gods agreed, though only if he could complete his task in six months. Impossible! He would fail, they thought, and the wall would at least be partway done, and for free.

"But ... with the aid of his horse, Svadilfari, the giant came near to success. So what did Loki do? He turned himself into a beautiful mare and lured Svadilfari away, not only saving Freya and the sun and the moon, but also thereafter giving birth to Sleipnir, finest of horses. And what, Sigurd, do you say to that?"

"Cheater."

Jari groaned and slumped forward over his pommel. "I give up."

"Aye, you should," said Halvar. "He slew you with a single word."

Morning was coming into the forest, the light falling golden on the tree trunks and lying between the shadows, when the hounds picked up a scent, running and belling as they followed the trail. The hunt master sounded his horn for deer, and the hunting party strung their bows. A shape flashed between the trees, and the men kicked their horses into a gallop, flying past the belling hounds, sailing over fallen trees and through gullies. Sigurd drew an arrow from his quiver as Gladung galloped up a rise, but the first shot must be the king's.

The stag vanished into the tangled underbrush. The hunters reined in, casting about until their quarry bolted into the open again. When the stag swung aside, offering his death, Ælf loosed an arrow. The stag screamed, but the arrow had missed its perfect mark; the beast stumbled on for a time before crashing into the deadfall.

They hunted through the morning, taking several red deer and some smaller game. Sigurd and Jari both loosed arrows upon an eight-point, and it fell dead. As the arrows were pulled from behind the shoulder, the men argued about whose had been the killing shot, but Sigurd said nothing.

When the sun was high, they stopped near a stream to water the horses and tether them for a rest. Sigurd dug into his saddlebags for the food he had brought and went to sit beside Jari. Jari might have sat with the other thanes who gathered around the king, but he knew that Sigurd would not sit with the other boys, and he did not like when Sigurd sat alone.

"It was a good shot," Jari conceded as Sigurd unwrapped the cloth from his buttered bread. "The eight-point, I mean."

"Yes. My arrow struck the heart."

Jari's red eyebrows climbed. "And mine didn't, is that what you're saying? Then why didn't you speak up?"

Sigurd shrugged. "I knew I killed him."

"And you didn't care what anyone else thought?"

Sigurd's gaze wandered to where the other boys, sons of thanes, sat together, laughing and eating, two of them arguing. "The truth is the truth. Bragging and trying to make yourself look like something doesn't change it."

"Ah, Sigurd," said Jari, shaking his head and cutting into a wedge of cheese, "I fear for you. You do not understand people."

Rarely did Jari speak so soberly, and it made Sigurd look at him. "Ælf says the same. Does it matter? I am ... only myself." Sigurd frowned, knowing this did not quite capture what he meant but unable to find better words.

"You are not only yourself. No man is. Your life is also the people around you—what they think, what they do."

"But what did it matter what anyone thought? The stag was dead, and there was no proving who killed him."

"I'm not talking about the stag, and do not tell me you don't care for the regard of others—because I see your face when you are first and best. It means something to you."

Annoyed, Sigurd shifted his attention to Ælf's company. The king and his thanes made a fine sight in their supple leathers and brightly dyed wools, all trimmed with fur or woven borders. Silver and gold flashed at their arms and necks and glinted among their braids, banded their scabbards and quivers. Then there was Regin: dark and quiet, like a shadow among them.

Yesterday, after Regin had come and gone from the edge of the training yard where Halvar had been drilling Sigurd in attack patterns, Sigurd had asked Halvar whether Regin had truly been the king's smith.

"He was smith here, sure enough," Halvar had said, "but that was in the time of King Knut, King Hjalprek's great, great, something great grandfather, or so Hjalprek told me."

"But how can Regin be so old? Where did he come from?"

"Who could know? He just was."

Halvar doggedly started the sequence again. Sigurd, distracted into forgetting the formal patterns, swept his sword in a fluid block and slipped outside of Halvar's range, causing the older man to stumble. As Halvar recovered himself, Sigurd pressed, "But ... who is he?"

Saying nothing of Sigurd's broken but effective pattern, Halvar sighed and said, "Fine, boy. But this is just hearth-talk, hear? The story goes that Regin came to the king's hall in rags, tattered and thin, a thing of pity they say, though how any could pity him with his eyes like chips of ice, I know not. Were he but a shivering heap, I think I would avoid him.

"It turned out he be a fine smith, and to work he went in the forge and soon earned his place. His weapons cut so sharp they could nearly sing upon the air, or so it be said. It's also said that he be a wizard, though such is always said of strange folk. They say too that he be as cunning as a wolf—and that I do not doubt. Now came a time when King Knut found himself in a terrible, bloody war. What hand Regin had in the winning of it, none could say, but after, King Knut gifted him a good deal of gold, and Regin left."

"The men called him Master of Masters," said Sigurd, fishing for more. "That first night in the hall. I heard it."

"Aye, they call him that, and the Counselor, too, for even kings bend to his words, or so it be said."

It amused Regin to be called a wizard. He knew firsthand what a wizard was, and he possessed none of that magic. What he had was wisdom and patience, and he had learned both by necessity. He could wait for his enemies to forget him, could wait for a king to die; he could outwait any man. But where there was opportunity, he wasted no time.

Regin watched Sigurd slip away from his companion. The boy was stealthy, ducking around to the far side of his horse and out of sight. But Regin, too, could be silent and quick. He reached the head of Sigurd's horse before the boy had finished tightening his saddle girth.

"Sneaking off?" asked Regin, and Sigurd's eyes flew to him. His face revealed his irritation at being taken by surprise. He needed to learn how to guard his expression.

Sigurd straightened a rein. "Jari knows where I'm going."

"And where is that?"

"I have some snares along this stream. I want to check them."

"Trapping is a fine method of hunting. It calls for patience and planning. Shall I ride with you?" Regin posed it as a question only because he knew Sigurd would say yes. The boy was intrigued by him, and not afraid. That pleased Regin mightily.

They rode side by side along the streambank, the fallen leaves brittle and noisy beneath their horses' hooves. A raven hopped along a branch overhead. Regin frowned at it. He did not like birds, for they chattered and meddled, and none more so than ravens. Perhaps the bird was only a bird, or perhaps it was one of Odin's creatures. Regin knew well the ways of gods, and the raven's presence made him wonder, just for a moment, whose will he was truly working.

When they had ridden some way, Regin said, "A strange thing it seems to me that a Volsung should come of age the thrall of a lesser man."

Sigurd scowled. "I am no thrall."

"What are you, then?"

"I am Hjal—I mean ... I am Ælf's ward."

"Ah. The Volsung wealth, too, must be his ward, then. A pleasing arrangement for him, I dare say." When Sigurd frowned and said nothing, Regin pressed, "What do you think of Ælf?"

"He is my mother's husband, and the king."

"You, too, are a king by right. Does it mean anything?" When Sigurd only frowned again, Regin gave him the answer. "It does not. Power has meaning. Power makes—and unmakes. Ælf has power. Do you know why?"

"He has land and men to fight for him."

"And gold."

"And gold," Sigurd agreed.

"But ... there is cunning, too. And patience. And prowess. And fear. There are many forms of power. They are not always visible, nor always immediate."

When they came to Sigurd's first snare, a rabbit lay panting and glassy-eyed with the leather noose around its body. "What is the matter?" Regin asked, seeing how Sigurd stiffened.

"This is the trouble with traps. They can be cruel."

"You do not like to see it suffer?"

Sigurd looked startled. "Of course not."

"Most do not notice others' suffering. Some delight in it." At Sigurd's look of disbelief, Regin said, "It is power made visible. You set this trap; it is yours. You caught this rabbit; its suffering is your doing. This is your power—made visible."

"But I do not delight in it."

Regin might have replied to that, might have told Sigurd how men learn to delight in such shows of power, but Sigurd had already swung down from his tall horse, so Regin let it go. Sigurd went to the snare and snapped the rabbit's neck. He did not flinch from killing, it seemed.

After Sigurd collected a second rabbit and a dark-pelted marten from his other traps, they returned to where the hunting party had rested and found them gone. Sigurd pointed to the trampled underbrush marking their path, though soon the belling of hounds was enough to guide their way. Then they heard the shouts of men and the screams of a wild boar. Gladung broke into a canter. Regin followed, watching Sigurd unlace his ash spear and pull it from under his leg.

Most of the hunting party was yet mounted, spears in hand, trying to fence in the hulking, waist-high boar for the men on foot. The hounds barked and snapped at the beast's short, thick legs as it ran squealing, its rounded back broad and bristled. One hound managed to catch an ear in its teeth. The boar's head bowed under the sudden weight, but it gave a quick upward thrust and caught the hound with a yellowed tusk. The hound let out a pained yelp and fell away from the struggle.

The boar reached the edge of the clearing and threw itself into a thicket. The hounds circled, barking and snapping as the boar pressed deeper into the dense brush. The hunt master tried to call them off, but the hounds were frenzied beyond obedience.

Ælf led the men on foot. He stopped within spear's reach of the boar, whose heaving sides were rustling the thicket. Daylight limned the end of its tapered snout, but the small eyes and thick, bristled body were hidden in the dark covering of brush.

Ælf shifted his spear, balancing it, sidestepping to get a view of the boar's neck. He stabbed into the thicket. With a scream of rage, the boar charged out. The men scrambled, several falling. A few stabbed at the boar as it barreled past.

The hounds flew after the beast, and the horses jibbed and pranced as their riders fought to hold the perimeter. Sigurd, who had halted there with Regin, urged Gladung past the other horses and into the boar's path. The old stallion jogged side to side, ready to leap out of the way. A boar's tusks could shred a horse's legs as easily as a man's.

As the boar veered left, Sigurd lunged out of the saddle, putting all his weight behind the spear. The point stabbed into the boar's neck and the beast crashed to the earth. Hands still on the spear, Sigurd was flung over its back.

The boar was dead by the time the men had swung off their horses and run to where it lay. Halvar hauled Sigurd to his feet, hunting for blood or broken bones. Others flew to the king where he stood dusty and bruised, the tear in his trouser leg showing how nearly the tusk had caught him, how close he had come to death or laming.

How lucky he was! the men exclaimed. "Indeed," Ælf agreed stiffly and congratulated Sigurd, stiffly, on his success.

Silence fell as the hunt master killed the gored hound. Then the men laughed about the fury of the boar and Sigurd's daring kill. Jari stood over the boar, marveling at the ash spear standing in its thick neck. "How in the name of Hel did you hit the spine in that mad leap?"

"Don't sulk, Jari," someone said. "He's better than you, that's all."

Jari grinned, not offended. "Well, no one doubted that. But it's not quite fair for the rest of us, is it, when the Volsung stands so tall among us—yet comes but to our elbows." The men objected to this absurd statement, measuring Sigurd's height and making much of his youthful prowess.

Regin looked on as the spear was pulled from the boar's dense flesh and returned to Sigurd. The boy set about cleaning it, clearly relieved to busy himself. He wasn't shy, Regin thought, simply uninterested in the talk. Unaware, too, of what his actions had done, blind to where his perfect spear thrust had struck most deeply: into his stepfather's pride. A few noticed and quieted their praise of the boy. Regin hid his smile.

※

Fall passed into winter, and the snows fell. Smoke rose continually from the roof vents, drifting over the white landscape. It was a time for mending clothes and gear, fletching arrows and telling stories. The food was heavy, the mead thick and sweet.

When the days lengthened again, men and women went out wrapped in furs to prepare for spring. By the time the snows were melting, training had resumed in the muddy yard, the animals were restless in their byres, and Regin deemed it time to speak.

The Mead Hall stood all but empty. A fire burned low in the day's warmth, casting dim light over Ælf and Regin's game of stones. There was a tradition in the north, which Regin had observed because it suited him: the greater the question, the longer one must abide with his host before asking it. By now, there could be no doubt that Regin wanted something—and very little doubt as to what that was. By now, Ælf would be ready to have it done with.

Regin said, "Your father was a fair hand at the board, but he had little gift for treachery."

"He could never have beaten you, then."

"Certainly not." Regin considered his pieces and set his trap.

He watched Ælf study the board, frowning with the quiet anger that Regin had come to see lay within him. Often through the winter, Regin had thought how he should have taken Ælf in fosterage. In the man's youth, Regin had been little impressed with his easy smile and practiced, charming manner and had not even asked Hjalprek for him. But Ælf had grown into a more sober man than expected. Life had hardened him.

Regin said, "Tell me of the boy."

"Sigurd?" asked Ælf, as though there could be any doubt, as though resenting the boy's prominence. "What of him? He'll be a warrior."

"Not just that, I think. His father was a king."

Ælf made a dismissive gesture. "Lygni yet holds the Volsung lands. It will take more than boyish daring to recover them. He'll need men, and in case you hadn't noticed, he's not exactly a natural leader."

Regin smiled his wolf-smile. "You seem to me a little young for such bitterness. Hjordis is not yet too old to bear you a son."

Ælf's laugh was sour. "After fourteen winters of barrenness, you imagine she'll quicken? No."

"At least the gods have blessed you with a fine stepson."

"Indeed. How generous they are." Ælf picked up his mead horn and frowned to find it empty.

As they played on, Ælf showed some cunning but not enough. Regin said, "You're right that he's no leader. But I wonder: will it matter? Even now, so many love him—as your father did. Sometimes men follow the sun despite its silence."

"They love his name," Ælf said.

Regin might have mentioned the boar hunt or any other story he had collected about the boy, but instead he said, "And what it promises."

"And what does it promise?"

Regin only looked upon the board and said, "Your move."

There were three moves Ælf might make to delay his defeat. He made one of them and sighed.

Regin countered him, near now to victory, and said, "I would foster him."

"His mother might object to that."

"He is not hers to keep."

"There have been other offers."

"Of course there have. He is the son of Sigmund, son of Volsung, descendant of Odin himself."

Ælf cast a hard look across the board at Regin. "What can it be to you, to foster boys of noble birth? You have no kingdom for which to build alliances. You are a smith."

More than that and Ælf knew it, but Regin did not protest. Some truths were more powerful left unspoken. Instead, he spoke a smaller truth. "I have much to teach."

"That is all? You want to teach?"

"As you say, I am a smith. I make things. One of those things is men."

"For what possible purpose ... Counselor?"

"A king wants to see his kingdom lay around him and know that he has shaped it. A skald wants to sing his stories where there are ears to hear them. A smith wants only to see his finely made gold flash in the sunlight."

"There is more to you than that."

"I am a smith," Regin reminded him, and Ælf scowled at his earlier words, not liking to have them wielded against him.

Regin relented, for there were times to wound a man's pride and times to salve it. He said, fingering Ælf's taken game pieces, "You are right, of course, for there is more to all men, including the Volsung. You must decide whether you prefer him under your roof—or mine."

Chapter Three

ÆLF INTENDED TO IGNORE Regin's words, but they grew in his mind, shadowed his thoughts—because they were his own, given voice. He watched the men at night, gathered around the hearth, telling tales of the Volsungs to please the boy. He watched Regin, haunting the hall as he had all winter, cloaking himself in silence while the men spoke too freely.

Then there was Hjordis. Who would never find him worthy. Who would never not see Sigmund when she looked upon her son.

She was to Ælf what she had always been: the young queen, stiff with dignity, standing upon the Volsung shore. She had been all the more beautiful for her sad eyes and hard mouth, for her fierceness when she took him to the cave where Sigmund's wealth was hid, seeming to dare him to bind himself to her with that treasure. Entering the cave's dark belly, a chill had crept over him, and when he had emerged, squinting in the sudden light and clutching a handful of golden trinkets, Hjordis had almost smiled at him, a pitying sort of smile, and held out her hand.

Her fingers had been smooth and fine under the flaking blood of her fallen lord, and Ælf had known at once that he would wed her. But in the years that followed, he often recalled the chill of that cave and saw that it had been a warning: what he chose there would always be dark and unfathomable to him.

He was sometimes too rough with her, because she made him feel so small. She always scorned him after, and thus it was a bad time to speak with her, but on this night, words felt like weapons, so he used them.

"Once the roads clear, Regin will leave. And Sigurd with him."

Ælf thought Hjordis might plead with him. He thought how good it would feel to hear her beg him for something, as he had so often begged for her love.

He was sitting up against the headboard. She was standing bare before the brazier's glowing coals, bathing from a silver bowl. The light painted pale orange over the curves of hip and breast. Every stroke of her cloth filled the air with cleansing rosemary.

When she said nothing, Ælf reminded her, "Sigurd would have been fostered years ago had my father not clung to him. He must be fostered now. How else can he learn to live in the world?"

"Why Regin?" was all she said.

She was putting him on the defense, as she always did, so he threw back, "Why not?"

"Whom does it serve to send Sigurd into obscurity, so far away?"

Ælf realized she was well prepared for this argument, that she had known it would come. He cursed women's wisdom, to see ahead of men.

"My father was fostered with Regin," Ælf reminded her.

Hjordis only gazed at him, her silence saying that he had not answered her question.

Ælf threw the blankets aside and stood from the bed. He went to her and smoothed a hand over her shoulder. She stiffened.

"Cold woman," he complained.

"What could you possibly want from me now?"

Ælf made a sound of anger and snatched up his tunic. He should rebuke her for her insolence, send her from the chamber in disgrace. He was the king—and her husband. But he pulled on his tunic and left the chamber himself. There were warmer beds and more welcoming arms, easier lovers.

As a boy, after his mother had died, Ælf had been surrounded by women intent upon his father's bed. He had had many mothers then, women both charming and solicitous, and he had learned to love and be loved by them. He had been a handsome youth and even now was a handsome man. He knew how to speak to women, how to touch them. He knew how they were meant to respond. He did not know why, then, he should care so much about the love of this one woman who refused it to him.

Regin saw how the king's gaze followed Hjordis when she passed through the hall, wrapped in her anger, that swanlike neck unyielding and her slender arms crossed tight against her chest. He saw Ælf, eyes red-rimmed, stare into his mead horn at night and forget the meat on his plate. Nothing killed like love. Regin had lived long enough to know the truth of that.

He also knew that if Ælf refused Sigurd to him, there would be no second chance. That was why he had kept one argument in reserve, a thing to say in larger company.

One evening, when the early spring rains were streaming off the roof and Hjordis had conceded to pour ale for the men, Regin lifted his cup to receive from her and spoke to no one and everyone. "I must soon leave, to prepare for my foster son."

Hjordis splashed ale over the rim of his cup. Pretending not to notice, Regin went on, "His name is Gunnar, and he is the oldest son of King Gjuki of Burgundy."

"Burgundy?" echoed Ælf, and Regin smiled, saying, "Aye. A rich kingdom, sitting fat along the Rhine."

Hjordis's fine hands tightened on the pitcher, and Regin almost pitied her. He had taken the last of her control over her husband's decision. With such a valuable foster bond in the bargain, Ælf could let the boy go and call it a favor to him.

So it proved. The next day, when Regin got his way, he said only, "You honor me, King of the Danes," and lowered his eyes to conceal his triumph.

During the weeks before Sigurd's departure, Ælf's household woke from its lingering winter stupor. Hjordis and her women worked their looms with sudden vigor, beating the weaving tight with their whale-bone batons. They cut the new cloth as well as cloth from their winter weaving, sewing fresh clothes for the queen's son. Hjordis spoke little to Ælf. She would never quite forgive him, and he would never know that her anger was really with Odin, who had set all this in motion. But Odin she could not punish, so she punished her husband instead.

On a day that broke clear and fine for traveling, Hjordis, Ælf, and the thanes gathered in the courtyard to see Sigurd off. Tension ran through the men. Many had wanted to form an escort, but Regin had refused. He would begin the boy's education while they traveled, he said, and could not do so with a large company. This made no sense to anyone, but Ælf had shrugged, weary of the whole matter. Halvar had begged Ælf to consider what his father would have thought of Sigurd traveling unprotected, of Ælf allowing it. Ælf had looked hard at his father's old friend and had said nothing.

Now, with the sun a handsbreadth above the horizon, Sigurd made his farewells with an unexpected pain. Until now, he had only been looking forward: to following in Hjalprek's footsteps, to adventure, to the mystery of Regin. Over the winter, Regin had often spoken with him, telling tales of the strangest splendors and dangers. Sigurd knew many stories of gods and heroes, but Regin spoke of other marvels: beautiful female creatures who haunted the waters of the south, luring men into the murky depths for love and death; faraway lands with no trees nor grass nor water, only sand and fiery spirits. Regin spoke, too, of the other realms branching from the world-tree, and Regin's tales transformed these places into greater wonders. Where Jotunheim, the realm of giants, had always been a mere battleground for the gods, Regin's telling gave it unbounded seas and magical forests and ancient mysteries. Regin made the world endless, and Sigurd thrilled at it.

Yet it was hard to have Halvar clap a hand to his shoulder and wish him well in a final sort of way, to hear Jari say, "How dull it's going to be without you." Then there was Hjordis.

She did not weep, though her weary eyes spoke of private grief, and she embraced her son fiercely. It startled him, for she had not embraced him in his entire memory. He did not know how to return the gesture, so he stepped back, confused. He instantly regretted that step away, for he could not step forward again. He said, "Goodbye, Mother," and felt, for a brief, searing moment, a terrible sense of loss.

Then Hjordis straightened, her fine jaw as firm as a man's. "Look after yourself, for no one else will."

Troubled, Sigurd turned to Ælf and made an easier parting. The leave-taking turned formal then, with Regin giving the required thanks to Ælf and the king returning the necessary courtesies. Sigurd busied himself with his horse, glad to have this one friend going with him.

As they rode through the town along the wood-paved way, Regin said nothing, but as they passed through the ramparts and out of the stronghold, the Danish banners flying above them, he remarked, "You did not look back. Was it pride?"

The question surprised Sigurd. "I don't know."

"Not pride, then. Why?"

Sigurd shrugged, at a loss and not wanting to speak of how it felt to leave. "The road is ahead."

"That is a good answer," said Regin.

It was not without reason that Ælf's thanes had wanted to escort Sigurd. The road was safe only within a day's ride of the king's stronghold, where his men carried out the law. Beyond that, travelers often fell prey to outlaws and other desperate men. Regin knew of these dangers but was not much troubled by them. His death had been foretold long ago, and it would not come at the hands of a stranger. Regin half believed it would not come at all. Traveling, then, did not much concern him.

Nothing happened at first. They traveled all day, spending their nights in the woods or in a farmer's steading. On a day of heavy rain, a sliver a hacksilver bought shelter and warm food. Sigurd passed that dull day in the farmer's barn, loosing his arrows again and again at a target he fashioned from a rotten barrel.

When all the arrow tips were dull, he realized the waste. Never before had he needed to think of such things. In the king's stronghold, fresh arrows had appeared in his quiver as though by magic, like Odin's arm-ring, Draupnir, which replicated itself every seven days in endless renewal.

When he confessed to Regin that he had dulled his arrows, Regin's icy blue eyes seemed to glitter with amusement in the light of the steading's cooking fire. "I wondered when you would figure that out."

"Practice matters," said Sigurd, repeating what he had often been told.

"So does practicality."

"What should I do?"

Regin withdrew a whetstone from his pack and handed it to Sigurd. "My gift to you."

When Sigurd had struggled a little while, Regin sighed and snatched both arrow and whetstone from him. "Watch," he said and demonstrated.

Regin's fingers were quick and clever, his precision mesmerizing. Sigurd lost himself in watching, noticing not the steading nor the family huddled apart from them on the other side of the fire.

When the farmer's young daughter let out a sudden cry, Sigurd's eyes jumped to her then followed her frightened gaze to Regin. The smith worked the whetstone before the fire, but the light played a strange trick with his shadow, warping it against the wall behind him. It shrank and shriveled him, stretching his arms to unnatural thinness and enlarging his hands on the tools. The shadow thrust the whetstone in Sigurd's direction, jolting his attention to the smith in the flesh, who looked as he always had.

"I've shown you," Regin said shortly. "It is your work to do."

Sigurd took the whetstone. He glanced at the wall again, but all looked as it should. The child had settled in her mother's arms, and the fire worked no more mischief that night.

They had made nearly a week's progress south before trouble found them. This trouble took the form of a thin, filthy man who emerged from the woods behind them and aimed a bow at their backs. His high, anxious voice demanded they drop their coins and ride on.

"There are two of us," Regin said without looking back. "Do you think you can kill us both before one of us kills you?"

"Just drop what you got! I killed someone before!"

Sigurd slowly drew his knife from his belt. His traveling cloak hid his intention but not his movement.

"Don't move!" the man shouted, bowstring creaking as he drew harder. "I'll shoot!"

Regin cast a sneering look over his shoulder. "How can he drop his money if he doesn't move?"

"Just do it slow! And don't look at me!"

"There is a thing you should know," said Regin, holding the man's attention as Sigurd readied his knife. "I saw Hel once, the death-goddess, when she came for a man not unlike you, a murderer. She had a beautiful face, certainly, golden and bright, with lips any man would long to kiss. That lying beauty serves its purpose, for you can almost forget she is a corpse from the waist down. But that is the truth of her: the putrid flesh of her legs, and her skeletal feet clacking over the stones with every step. But you need not the sight of her, nor the sound of her clicking toes, to know she is coming for you. You need only test the air—" Regin sniffed loudly. "—for the stink of rot."

Though the words were not for him, they froze Sigurd as much as they did the outlaw, and both of them jumped when Regin shouted, "Sigurd, now!"

Sigurd spun Gladung and flung his knife, but much claimed his attention: Regin's words, for one, and also the sorry sight of the man. Ragged clothes hung off his thin frame, much like Hel's rotting flesh, and his matted hair and beard obscured his face. But the would-be robber was also distracted, and the arrow he loosed flew wide into the woods. That same instant, Sigurd's blade slashed his thin cheek. With a cry, the man dropped his bow to clutch at the wound. He fled into the trees.

Sigurd walked Gladung to where his knife had stuck in the mud. He dismounted, boots squelching. After cleaning the blade on his cloak, he returned it to his belt. He regarded the crudely made bow. "What should we do with it?"

"Break it," said Regin. "It's no use to anyone but outlaws."

Sigurd broke the bow over his knee and tossed the pieces into the woods. He remounted, his boots now muddy in the stirrups, and nudged Gladung into a trot to catch up with Regin, who had started down the road.

"Why did you not kill him?" Regin asked as Gladung settled to a walk beside his own black horse.

"I missed the mark."

"On purpose?"

"I'm not sure."

Regin's icy eyes narrowed on Sigurd. "Consider the consequences of your mercy. That man might have shot me, or you. In sparing him, you've given him the chance to rob, and perhaps kill, someone else." He paused. "Do you see this truth?"

"Yes, Regin."

"What is it, boy? You're thinking something."

"Only that he was so poor and desperate."

"That only makes a man more dangerous. Too great a wanting can lead only to wickedness. Every man learns this, if he lives long enough."

After the day's trouble, Sigurd was glad to lodge under a roof that evening, even though the steading was a small, poor place, the meal nothing more than barley cooked in watery broth.

When the trenchers had been wiped clean and stacked on a low shelf, the farmer's two sons were sent to sleep in the barn, then he and his wife set about their evening tasks. The farmer mended a broken halter, sewing a new leather strip to the crownpiece with a bone needle. His wife spun undyed wool, the distaff held in the crook of her arm and the spindle sinking again and again to the floor, drawing out the thread in silence. Sigurd busied his hands with Regin's whetstone while Regin stared into the fire, busy with his thoughts. Sigurd looked for strangeness in Regin's shadow, but it flickered against the wall in the shape of the man hunched before the fire, and Sigurd's memory of the eerie, shrunken image the other night seemed almost a dream.

"What, boy?"

Sigurd startled, having thought Regin too preoccupied to notice his attention. After glancing at the farmer and his wife, who had settled on their pallets, backs to the fire, snores marking their sleep, he asked, "Did you really see Hel?"

"Only the shameful dead see Hel."

Disappointment snagged Sigurd's heart. "So you didn't see her, then?"

The firelight glinted off Regin's eyes. He seemed to consider his answer. "I dreamed of her once."

"What was the dream?"

Regin was silent for a time then said, "There is one man I hate above all. I dreamed of his death—and that Hel came for him. But whether it was a dream of wanting or of truth, I do not know."

Sigurd asked cautiously, "And who is this man?"

"No one for you to be concerned about right now."

"But what did he do?"

"Murder," Regin said. "Many murders but one quite dreadful, for he killed his own father."

"His own father?" Sigurd echoed in horror.

"For greed and gold did he commit his crime."

"That is terrible."

"Aye." Regin never lifted his eyes from the fire. "Go to sleep, Sigurd. And stop ruining that knife."

Their next day's travel ended without a village in sight, and they camped a short way into the woods. "Sigurd," said Regin with sudden heaviness. "A man who goes through this life always guided and protected is a man who lives for others, in the shelter and shadow of others. Do you want to be such a man?"

Sigurd swallowed hard on his mouthful of bread and dried fish smeared with butter. "No, Regin."

"Such a man is not free," Regin went on as the firelight played over the sharp planes of his face. "He is dependent. He is nothing of his own. You do not want that?"

"No."

Regin held out his next words like a honey cake. "It is easier, though. Safer. More comfortable." He eyed Sigurd, but the boy only frowned at him, unmoved by that, waiting for the point. A smile played around Regin's mouth. "You think you want to be more, but here is a thing: all men believe that about themselves. Precious few have the will for it."

Regin fell silent, waiting for protest and bluster, waiting for Sigurd to claim that he was different, as all men liked to claim. Sigurd said nothing. Almost, Regin worried. Did the boy did not understand that he was being challenged, his strength questioned? More than once, Regin had wondered if Sigurd's mind was slow. Such a failing would try his patience, but even a dull sword could kill if swung hard enough. Almost, Regin would prefer that to the other possibility: that Sigurd's stillness hid depths beyond his knowing. Sometimes the boy's eyes looked as clear and empty as the blue sky—and sometimes they looked as dark and deep as the unfathomable sea.

Sigurd's silence left Regin no choice but to go on. "We must both learn the truth of your will. Struggle, you see, strengthens a strong will—and breaks a weak one. But do you know what *will* even is?"

Sigurd frowned in a way that said he had never thought about it before. But, then, most grown men had not either. They thought simply: strength—and found a way to tell themselves that they had it.

"Will, Sigurd, is taking a path, holding to it even in the face of toil and trouble and doubt and pain. One cannot keep to a path without knowing where they are going and why they want to get there. Do you understand?"

Sigurd frowned again, plainly trying, and said, "I think so."

"Experience will teach you what words cannot. Now listen closely, boy, mark me well. My house is known, when you get near enough, and not difficult to find. From here, the journey takes you south across the river Elbe, then south and west to the West Plain, and the river valley there."

"Regin—"

"Across the Elbe. Then south and west to the West Plain and the river valley. Repeat it to me."

"Regin—"

"Repeat it to me."

"Across the Elbe. South and west to the West Plain. To the river valley."

"Again."

"Across the Elbe then south and west to the West Plain and the river valley. But, Regin—"

"That is all I have to say."

"Regin, I don't—"

"I will not speak to you again," said Regin and turned his face toward the fire and his own path.

Chapter Four

THERE IS A PARTICULAR quality of silence, a settled feel to the world, that marks solitude. When Sigurd woke in the morning, he recognized it at once. He sat up on his bedroll. At the movement, ravens stirred in the branches overhead. Sigurd looked to where the horses had been tethered. Gladung was sniffing through the dead winter grass for new spring shoots, and he was alone.

Sigurd's heart skipped, his body knowing what his mind could not yet comprehend. Slowly, he rose and, slowly, he walked around the camp. He scanned the trees, dim in the early light, quiet in the way of the untroubled woods.

He went to Gladung. The horse nudged his chest in his usual way of greeting, and usually Sigurd was braced for it. This time it caught him off guard, and he stumbled back. He looked around again.

"Wh ..." He did not finish the word. It might have been what or why or where, but in any case it did not matter, for the answer was clearly that Regin was gone.

Sigurd had known that Regin's speech last night had meant something, but he hadn't known what, and he still could not quite believe it. But then, Sigurd had never been betrayed before, and the idea of betrayal is incomprehensible until it has happened.

Sigurd saddled Gladung, for there was nothing else to do. As he secured his bedroll and saddlebags, his stomach growled a reminder. He dug for the pouch of dried fish and found more than had been there before, food that Regin must have put there. His heart sank at this confirmation of abandonment.

When he and Gladung emerged from the woods, Sigurd looked back the way he had come then forward to where he had been going. He guided Gladung onto the road, turning south toward Regin.

Last night Regin had spoken of strength and will and following a path. Across the Elbe, he had said, then south and west to the West Plain and the river valley. Regin meant for him to travel alone, meant for him to prove that he could. But, Sigurd soon remembered as the familiar rhythm of Gladung's walk settled him, he did not mind being alone, and the road lay clear before him.

The night was harder. He woke at every sound and half-sensed movement. Once, he thought he saw someone. But it was only moonlight falling on a gnarled tree, not on a craggy, bearded face. It was a sweep of mossy shadow, not a cloak. It was a rustle of wings and nothing more.

Another day passed and another night, and the road went on and on over the plains and through forests and past dull little villages. He sought no shelter in steadings, for he did not enjoy the company of strangers or the smoky stink of their cooking fires. He preferred the woods with the occasional sightings of deer and hawks and silent foxes. He liked the scents and sounds and having Gladung nearby, and he learned to sleep soundly amid unfamiliar trees.

Not having stopped to talk to anyone, Sigurd did not realize how close he had drawn to the Elbe. It would not have meant anything to him anyway, for he did not know that a river crossing was a place of opportunity, nor that a place of opportunity was a place of trouble.

One night, Sigurd was startled into waking, his shout stifled by the hand clamped over his mouth. He lunged for his knife but too late; he was yanked off the ground. His feet kicked out at nothing.

"What'd you wanna to wake 'im for?" someone complained from nearby. In the faint moonlight, Sigurd could just make out the form of a short, slight man. "We take the horse and go, quiet-like. You agreed to it, Feng."

"But we can sell 'im, see? I could get a new pair of shoes."

Sigurd wrenched hard, but the huge arms caged him tight, clamping him against a paunchy belly. The greasy hand locked over his mouth stank of onion.

"You say we'll sell 'im, but don't think I've forgotten what happened last time." The other man spat in disgust. "And look at this horse, you fool, it's a quality animal. And his things? He can't be out here alone, and even if he is, a fancy boy like this? Someone might come after 'im, and that means after *us*."

"But, Rik," the man called Feng pleaded, "there's no one around. We waited. You said it was safe."

"Safe *here*. At his campsite, you wool-brain." Rik shook his head. "Well, we can't have 'im run off to tell someone. You woke him, you deal with 'im."

As Rik turned away, Sigurd bit the oily hand clamped over his mouth and slammed his heel down on his captor's foot. Feng yelped, losing his grip. Sigurd wrenched away and bolted into the woods.

He didn't know which of them caught him, was aware only of his tunic seizing tight as a fist grabbed it, of himself weightless as he was yanked off his feet, of the flash of light and burst of pain as his head struck the ground.

Sigurd woke tied to a tree. The rope bound his arms behind him, as though he hugged the tree at his back. His head swam nauseatingly. The men lay nearby, maybe sleeping, maybe not. Sigurd twisted his hands, seeking any give in the rope. The light rasping sound had Feng rolling to his feet. Sigurd's heart skipped as the big man crouched before him.

"You're not getting away." Foul breath washed Sigurd's face. "You should be nice to me. You should say you're sorry for biting me." When Sigurd said nothing, Feng's hand clamped his thigh in a bruising grip. "Say you're sorry!"

Sigurd held himself still and silent—until Feng groped between Sigurd's legs; that was too much. Sigurd kicked hard into Feng's groin. Howling, the big man grabbed Sigurd by the throat with one hand and pinched his genitals with the other, pinning him to the tree. Sigurd could do nothing but choke out a sound of pain and horror and helplessness.

"Hel's tits, man, leave 'im be."

"He won't say he's sorry!" Feng spluttered as Rik climbed, grumbling, to his feet. "He better say he's sorry or I'm gonna—"

Rik set the tip of a knife to Sigurd's temple. "I ain't watching that. Let 'im go, Feng, or I kill 'im." When Feng's hands sprang open, Sigurd hauled a breath into his lungs and yanked his knees to his chest. "Get back, ya fleabag." Rik stood there, the knife scratching sharply at Sigurd's temple, until Feng crept away and curled up on the ground like a scolded dog.

By the time the sun rose, Sigurd had fallen into an uneasy doze. He roused as Rik untied him from the tree. The light revealed sandy hair in matted braids and an unkempt beard. A bow hung at the man's back.

"You cause trouble and I'll let 'im have you. I just want money, but Feng … he's not right in the head. He likes boys like you. Blond. Pretty. You understand what I'm saying? Eh!" Rik slapped Sigurd's cheek. "You simple or what?"

"I understand." Sigurd's voice rasped through his bruised throat.

Rik's small eyes tracked over Sigurd. "Where you from? Why you alone? That sword of yours is right fine, and that's no farmer's horse you ride." He flicked Sigurd's fur-trimmed cloak with a grimy fingernail. "Very rich indeed. What's your name, boy?"

"You have taken my things. You cannot have my name."

Rik grinned, displaying rotting teeth. "Afraid I'll curse you with my dying breath? You been listening to too many stories, boy."

The outlaws wrestled Sigurd into Gladung's saddle, tying him down to the horse's neck and binding his hands at his back. Gladung pranced nervously, aware that something was wrong but trained to obey the reins no matter who held them. The pommel punched into Sigurd's stomach. "Hush, Gladung," he whispered painfully against the horse's rigid neck, and the old stallion settled a little.

This near the river crossing, the road was wide and well-traveled. They walked through the trees about twenty paces from it, keeping it in sight while they themselves could not easily be seen. Around midday, they heard voices as three riders approached. Sigurd drew breath to shout. He managed only a loud but inarticulate sound before Rik clamped a hand over his mouth. The travelers halted.

"Did you hear that?" asked one, and the men looked around, drawing their knives.

"It's another ten miles to the ferry," said another, urging his horse onward, eager to be gone. "We should ride. These woods are crawling."

The travelers kicked their horses into a canter. When they were out of sight, Rik released Sigurd's mouth to snatch his hair, bending his neck back as far as the bindings would allow.

"You think they were going to save you?" Rik laughed sourly. "They had their own skins to think of. Risk themselves for you? No, my boy. That ain't how the world works."

The day dragged by with Sigurd slumping numbly over Gladung's neck. Always one of the outlaws held the reins, even when they stopped to eat Sigurd's provisions. They offered him nothing. When Sigurd had to relieve himself, Feng looped a rope around his neck and stood beside him with a hand on his shoulder. Sigurd had no choice but to endure the hot, clenching fingers. But when the fingers began to creep, when

Feng let out an awful whine, Sigurd bolted, forgetting the rope around his neck.

The rope caught. Sigurd was yanked off his feet. Feng was on top of him before he could react, a sweaty, stinking mass of heaving flesh. Sigurd struck out with fists and feet, but blows rained down upon him, striking his torso and face until the world went black.

When Sigurd regained consciousness, he was again in the saddle, again tied down with his hands bound behind him. His head spun sickeningly, and he vomited down Gladung's shoulder.

"Get 'im some water," Rik ordered from somewhere ahead. "He's no use hauling around if he ain't worth selling. And what'd you swear, Feng?"

"That I won't hurt 'im again," muttered Feng. To Sigurd he whispered, "I didn't mean to. I forget sometimes. I want you to like me, see? I want us to be friends."

Feng untied Sigurd from Gladung's neck and shoved him upright. Sigurd would have gone over backwards had Feng not dropped the reins to catch him. Feng fumbled the waterskin from the saddlebag then reached up with it.

"See?" he said, his soft belly pressing against Sigurd's leg as he splashed water near Sigurd's mouth. "Friends, right?"

Sigurd rammed his knee into Gladung's side. Head finally free, Gladung spun at the pressure, haunches slamming into Feng. The big man fell with a cry of surprise. Sigurd shouted, and the old stallion leaped forward.

A bowstring twanged. An arrow thunked. Gladung stumbled but ran onward, ran and ran—until the danger was far behind, until the breath was gone from his body, until the road of his life had ended. Then the stallion crashed to the forest floor, throwing Sigurd from the saddle.

The world spun and tumbled and rolled. When Sigurd's body stopped, his mind yet sloshed like water in a jug. He retched again. Then he breathed in the soil and the woods and felt, finally, the stillness of it all. It was from that stillness that he knew, even before he turned, that Gladung was dead.

He crawled on his knees, hands yet bound behind him, to the old stallion. Gladung's mouth was open, the bit yet between his teeth, the lather of his final run upon his chest—and an outlaw's arrow standing behind the girth. Sigurd leaned against the huge, still body and wept.

When he could collect himself, he worked his way to the saddlebags, fumbling with his bound hands until he got hold of his knife. Kneeling, he clamped the blade upright between his feet and sawed behind himself. At last the bloodied rope fell away, and he rolled his aching shoulders. His face hurt, and it was hard to swallow with his throat so bruised. His groin hurt too, but he didn't think about that.

He slid the knife into his boot then drew his sword from its scabbard and laid it to hand. He pulled his bow from its leather case and strung it. At least these had been on the horse. Much had, really. Except for the coins that Rik had transferred to his own pouch, the outlaws had left everything for Gladung to carry.

When night fell, deep and chill, and there was nothing but the dark woods and the dead horse, Sigurd built a fire. If it led the outlaws to him, so be it. He would not be asleep this time. He would not be unarmed and naïve and foolish. He would not be taken again. Almost, he hoped they would come so he could prove this.

Late in the night, the moon rose. Its light spilled down through the trees, and a dark shape moved among the shadowy pattern of branches. Taking up his sword, Sigurd stood and called out, "Show yourself, coward."

An old man wandered from the dark woods into the firelight, leaning on a gnarled staff, his cloak hanging from stooped shoulders and a wide-brimmed hat slouching low over one eye. "I have been called many things," he said in a deep, thoughtful voice, "but never that."

Chapter Five

"WOULD YOU SHARE YOUR fire with an old man?" asked the stranger, leaning on his staff as though world weary.

Recalling his manners, Sigurd said, "Please warm yourself, grandfather," and laid aside his sword, gesturing an invitation toward the bedroll he had been sitting on.

The old man walked with his staff striking out before him, and the firelight moved over it strangely, at one moment dancing along its humble, knotted length, at another seeming to pick out runes etched into a polished shaft. Above the staff, light flashed in a thin line, as though a blade were there to reflect it. But there was nothing.

The old man seated himself on Sigurd's bedroll. His toes were as gnarled as the staff he laid at his side, and the dust of his travels crusted his sandals and dark robe. Though his hat concealed much of his face, a long white beard lay against his chest, and the firelight played over a grim mouth.

"You've had a hard day, I think," said the old man.

Sigurd settled himself in the grass, but his throat tightened and he found he could not answer.

The old man held his knotted hands out to the fire to warm them. "Will you tell me what happened?"

"My horse died," replied Sigurd. "He died to save me."

The stranger cocked his head, regarding Sigurd from under the brim of his hat. "That is what happened?"

"Yes, grandfather."

The old man waited for a time, as though Sigurd must have more to add, then he said, "I see. Your horse died a good death, then."

"I did not want him to die at all."

"All things die, my son, some better than others." They watched the fire for a time, then the wanderer asked, "Would you share your bread with an old man?"

Sigurd jumped to his feet, ashamed of his poor manners. "What little I have, I would give to you, grandfather."

He went to his saddlebags, which he had drawn away from Gladung's body, and returned to the fire with what the outlaws had not eaten of his food.

"You do not have much," observed the old man.

"I lost some things today."

"Aye. Not just food, I think, nor your horse."

Sigurd did not know what he meant, so he simply held out the food in offering. The old man took a piece of stale bread and a wedge of cheese and a sliver of dried fish. Sigurd set the rest at his sandaled feet.

"Where are you going?" asked the old man. His portion had vanished, though Sigurd had not seen him eat it.

"I was on my way to my foster father."

"And now you are not?"

Sigurd was silent for a time. Then, "Things are not as I thought. Men are ... bad."

"Yes," said the wanderer. "Darkness lives in every heart."

"Not in animals."

"In animals, too. Have you not seen one horse drive another from the hay? Two dogs fight over a scrap of meat? They, too, know greed and glut."

"But ..." Sigurd looked back at the still mound of Gladung's body.

"Light shines only in the darkness," said the old man. "Nobility exists only amid the common meanness of man and beast. Because there was darkness to shine against, your horse died in greatness. Men do too, sometimes. But suffering comes with it."

"Is it always so?"

"From the first thawing of the ice, from the birth of the world—yes." He added, "Some men shatter against such hard truth."

Sigurd did not notice the tone of question in the wanderer's words, nor did he notice the way a single eye looked out from under the wide-brimmed hat. He was gazing into the web of moonlight woven through the dark woods. He had looked out to think, but thought fled at the sight of an unexpected wonder.

"What do you see?" asked the old man.

"Something. In the distance."

The moonlight shone against a smooth surface. The base of a wall, it seemed, one of gigantic proportions. Like the wanderer's staff, the image was uncertain, there but not, two truths in one: this wood—and another. Then came the forlorn howl of a far-off wolf. Its voice pierced the night with loneliness and pain and an eerie, exquisite beauty.

Sigurd did not realize he had risen until the wanderer clamped a hand on his elbow and commanded, "Stay."

"Did you hear the wolf, grandfather?" Sigurd swayed toward it, held back only by the strong, old hand.

"Oh, yes. I hear it."

"It is ... sad."

The wanderer sighed, weary and grim. "Yes, for long and long has the wolf been bound with the strength of mountains and the strange ways of wild things."

"Can we not do something, grandfather?"

The wanderer relaxed his grip on Sigurd's arm. "Would you, if you could? In loosing him, you would work good and evil with one hand."

Sigurd looked out with fevered eyes. "I do not know."

"Then you are not ready for that mystery. Stay. Let the world of men be enough for now."

Sigurd shivered and sat, and the vision of the wall faded from the moonlit woods, and the howl of the wolf was gone. There was only the crackling fire and the vaulted ceiling of tree branches to make a chill, wild hearth in the woodland.

The stranger said, "You are ill, my son. You should sleep."

Sigurd remembered then the knife in his boot and the sword at his side and the reasons for them. "I must keep watch, grandfather. There are men who might return."

"I will watch over you, this one night, and in the morning you must decide upon your path."

Then the old man reached out a knotted finger and traced a rune on Sigurd's forehead. When Sigurd slumped to the ground, deep in sleep, two ravens glided down from the branches above and settled on the wanderer's shoulders, watching the night with him.

Sigurd woke with the sun in his eyes. It slipped between the tangled branches and seeped through the bright leaves fanning out from their buds. He sat up, stiff and aching. His head was clear, the nausea gone, but his face hurt. When he touched it, the skin felt puffy and hot on one side. At first he could not think where he was or why. Then he remembered.

The fire had burned out, and there was no sign of the old man. Almost, it seemed a dream, a thing that had happened out of time and place; not just the visit, but the vision of the wall in the woods and the mournful cry of the wolf. But the morning's chill and Gladung's stiff body were real enough.

Sigurd stared into the ashes as he ate stale bread and salty cheese, swallowing hard against the dryness. He wished he had not lost his waterskin in his escape.

He did not think on the details of what had happened. He thought only on what he should do. As when Regin had left him, it was go forward or go back. But now he knew how hard the way was, and now he understood that Regin had betrayed him.

Regin would spend a hundred words on the decision. He had spent more than that trying to prepare Sigurd for it. But Sigurd needed none of that. He needed only to realize: I will not go back, so I will go forward.

Still, it was hard to go forward without Gladung. It was hard to leave him in the woods unburied, unburned, for scavengers to ravage, but there was nothing to be done about it.

Sigurd sorted through his gear for what he most needed and could carry. He stripped the saddle of its valuable silver stirrups, its rings and buckles. He packed these and the bridle into his saddlebags along with the remainder of his food.

Because the saddle itself had worth but was too cumbersome to carry, he buried it. His sword made an awkward spade, good only for cutting and loosening the earth. Mostly, he dug with his hands, which were soon thick with spring mud. It was worth the effort and the abuse of his sword, however, to not leave anything for the profit of roaming outlaws.

Then he tied his bedroll to his saddlebags and slung them over his shoulder, along with his quiver of arrows. He belted his sword at his waist and carried his bow. Thus burdened, he was sweating by the time he found the road. His ankle had been hurt in Gladung's fall, so even the road was hard going. In the afternoon, a man with a cart overtook him. At the offer of a ride, Sigurd hesitated, untrusting, but the man's ruddy cheeks and grey beard and the weary, well-mannered horse persuaded him.

The man would accept no payment but exacted a price with his endless chatter and questions. Where was Sigurd from? Where was he going? What had happened to him? Sigurd's vague answers never failed to remind the man of a story of his own, which he would launch into with a thousand words and forget his questions. On one point only did he really press Sigurd: a boy should not be on the road alone.

"I mean to say! Look at you! You've had trouble already. You must know it's not safe. Where is your father?"

"He is dead," Sigurd answered bluntly, and the man fell into a rare silence.

They reached the river near dusk and caught the last ferry to the town on the other side. While the man with the cart chatted with the ferryman, Sigurd slumped on the water-stained planks in exhausted relief. The bob and pull of the ferry, the splashing of the Elbe—these signaled the end of the first part of his journey. South and west he must now go, to the West Plain and the river valley, and to Regin. But first, he needed a horse.

When the ferry docked, Sigurd slipped away from the man with the cart and found a cheap inn where men were crowded around a smoky hearth fire, drinking from clay cups and eating from wooden trenchers, trading news. The innkeeper accepted a copper bead from Gladung's bridle in exchange for a place on the floor and a trencher of meat.

Sigurd hated the stink of bodies and the crude speech and the way too many eyes rested upon him. He did not know if those who stared were scheming or simply curious, but he wanted nothing to do with any of it. He rolled up in his cloak by the wall and hugged his belongings to him. It was long before he slept. When he did, he dreamed.

He was sitting beside the holding grave, where Hjalprek's body had been kept before the burning. He wanted to ask

Hjalprek something, though he wasn't sure what; he felt only the burn of a vital, unanswered question. The stone began to roll away from the entrance. The hand pushing it, however, was not the king's hand. It was softer, dimpled at the knuckles, the fingernails ragged and filthy. Sigurd recoiled as the outlaw Feng stepped from the holding grave.

In the way of dreams, the scene shifted, and Sigurd found himself running through a forest, away from some monstrous, unidentified thing. But no matter how hard he ran, he moved with agonizing slowness. Through the trees, he saw a horse. At first he thought it was Gladung, but it was white, and it moved with such speed that its legs blurred and doubled. Then a hand closed on Sigurd's shoulder, the fingers tight and hot and horrible. Terror seized him, and he fell to the ground, screaming without sound, under a smothering weight.

Sigurd jolted awake. He lay rigid, his heart racing. Then the sounds of snoring came to him, and the stink of unwashed bodies and burned food, and he felt the deadness of confined air. He remembered where he was and pressed harder against the wall, pulling his cloak tight. He did not sleep again that night.

The next morning, Sigurd sought out the merchants and horse traders. He sold his bridle and stirrups and the silver pieces from his saddle. They cheated him, but there was little he could do about it. He needed a horse. There was none like Gladung along the traders' picket lines, not that anything so fine could have been bought for the price of stirrups. He had to settle for a broad-backed roan gelding that was quiet enough to ride without a saddle.

Riding south and west, he passed through forests and over heaths and struggled through bogs with the sluggish gelding. Sometimes there were roads, in areas where some petty king or chieftain kept order. In such places, causeways were to be found, and Sigurd would ride with relief over the raised planks or gravel that stretched through some sticky, treacherous marsh. Between smaller towns, muddy tracks were more common. Often, there was only wilderness.

He rode through near-constant drizzle and killed what game he could find. The spring-scruffy furs he traded for bread or lodgings when he reached a town or settlement, for he had learned to find shelter and ask directions where he could. Where there was nothing but trees or vast stretches of scrubby heath, he tethered the horse and slept wrapped in his cloak. Sometimes dry kindling was to hand for a fire, often not.

One night, camped in a thin grove, Sigurd awoke to the sound of movement in the underbrush. He quietly drew his knife from his boot and listened to the hesitant creep of footsteps as he lay in his cloak as though dead asleep. The steps sneaked toward the pile of gear behind his head.

Sigurd sprang up. The would-be thief cried out and tried to scramble away, but Sigurd's knife plunged into his groin. As the man fell with a scream, Sigurd wrenched the knife free and slashed it across the man's throat. Warm blood sprayed from the wound.

Chest heaving, heart racing, Sigurd scrubbed a sleeve across his blood-flecked face. With a shaking hand, he wiped the blade clean against the man's clothes then slid it back into his boot. Grabbing the man's arms, he dragged the heavy weight away from his camp.

He washed his hands in the nearby stream, grateful to have camped this night near water, and returned to his bedroll. He lay sleepless, his hands jittery against his chest. A question scratched at him: had he done right? He pushed it away. In the morning, he untethered his horse and rode on without looking at the body. The question came back to him, but in daylight and with the deed behind, he thought easily, Yes.

All things die, the wanderer had said. *Some better than others.* It was each man's responsibility to set the course of his own death.

The moon had waxed and waned again before Sigurd drew near enough to Regin's that his name made folk wary. The wizard? they would say. What could you want of him? Stay away, they would advise. Go home. Then he began to hear, Aye, the river valley. Just south of the Glittering Heath.

Sigurd had never before heard of the Glittering Heath, and none could tell him anything except that it was a bad place, a dead place, a weirdly shimmering place. Stay away, they said, go home.

One evening, Sigurd sat with a farmer and his wife at their hearth, eating a portion of the rabbits he had killed and traded for shelter. He asked if they knew of Regin and where to find him. With no clear road, he must always adjust and refine his course.

The farmer stopped chewing and rolled a wary eye at Sigurd. "The wizard?"

Sigurd had heard this enough times to simply say, "Yes."

"His home be near, four days' ride. Good rich soil in the river valley, they say, though none will farm it but the wizard. It be in the very shadow of the Glittering Heath."

"Stay away from there, boy," advised the farmer's wife, pouring weak ale. "That place be cursed something terrible, to glitter and shine like a thing unnatural." She shuddered. "Go home, boy."

"What is the curse?" asked Sigurd, for this was the first he had heard the word used.

"An old curse, a curse of fire," she said. "Or so the stories say."

"What stories? Tell me."

"A monstrous fire," said the farmer. "Long, long ago. Something evil did bring it, though none dared speak of it for so long that now no one knows."

Sigurd stopped at no more farms, for the lush river valley soon revealed itself, the river flowing wide and placid through a gentle landscape. The fertile land should have been busy with crops and grazing animals. But it was true, as the farmer had said, that there were no people.

For two days, Sigurd rode along the river, catching fish and forcing sputtering fires from driftwood. The rains had eased, the sky clearing to blue. As one afternoon's shadows stretched into evening, he followed a bend in the river. The southern shore stood higher here, sloping steeply from the water, and as he rode around the bend, a building came suddenly into view on that high shore. The building crowned the slope, its roof stark against the blue sky—and strangely cluttered with irregular shapes. One lifted into the air, wings fanning wide. Birds, perched along the roof ridge.

Another movement caught Sigurd's eye. Where a wooden bridge spanned the water, someone was walking out to meet him.

As Sigurd drew near, Regin regarded him with pale, glittering eyes, though his smile was full and pleased. "So," he said, "you have come."

Chapter Six

REGIN TOOK IN SIGURD'S worn, travel-stained clothing and the bare-backed, stodgy roan that spoke of his troubles. He eyed the new pink scar on Sigurd's left cheek. The scar would fade, but the memory might not. "You know something of the world now," he said.

"Yes," Sigurd replied.

"How did you decide on your path?"

"I did not want to go back."

Such simplicity. "Why not?" When Sigurd frowned as though he had not really thought about it, Regin prodded, "You did not want to be like a horse-boy to a lesser king, a beggar in his hall?"

Sigurd's face darkened. "No."

"Then let us make you into something else."

As Regin led Sigurd over the bridge and up the path to the house, he watched the boy's eyes range over the twisted carvings along the roof peaks, over Lofnheith's birds. A blue-grey falcon circled, screeching.

"Why do they gather there?" asked Sigurd.

"My sister has a strong will."

This clearly startled the boy. "Your sister?"

"They are her birds."

"They just ... stay? And the hawks don't kill the songbirds?"

"As I said, she has a strong will."

They entered the packed-clay yard and Sigurd slid off the roan, pulling his saddlebags down from where they had rested on the horse's withers. His gaze traveled from the stable to the dairy and other buildings, then past the wattle fence to the green pastures and cropland.

"This is so remote," Sigurd observed. "Yet many men must work here."

Eight, in fact, outcasts, guilty of murder or other malice, but Regin knew how to manage them. He said simply, "I make use of those who come to me."

Hama emerged from the stable. Without a word, the wiry old man took the reins and led the animal away.

Regin led Sigurd along the gravel path to the stone porch steps and up to the door. The boy seemed inclined to linger over the door's swirling ironwork, but Regin ushered him inside.

In some ways, the house looked like any other. The central hearth was a raised square of dressed stones, where a fire burned under a blackened iron cooking pot set atop an iron rack. A few chairs stood about, a table, some cushions and baskets. The floor was spread with fresh rushes. But there was its strange emptiness and there was the owl, its pale face swiveling in the rafters.

"This chamber will be yours," said Regin, opening one of the doors that lined the west side of the house, calling Sigurd's attention away from the owl. "Once you've cleaned up, come eat."

Soon after, with the curling ends if his hair still dark from washing, Sigurd sat across the hearth fire from Regin. Steam curled from the fat-bellied pot, and the scents of lamb and garlic made Sigurd's mouth water. Turning a clay cup of warmed mead in his hands, Sigurd glanced up at the owl. The hearth light reached the heavy talons curling over a rafter but faded against the large, pale body.

Regin, weary of the boy's silence, prompted, "You are not angry."

"About what?"

Regin shook his head. "I cannot tell if you are a young fool or wise beyond your years. For leaving you, of course."

"Oh. I guess I am not angry, no."

"But you lost your horse. I thought he meant something to you."

"He meant a great deal to me. And I did not lose him. He died."

Regin ladled stew into a trencher. "And you do not blame me for that?"

Sigurd's eyes grew distant as he stared into the fire. "All things die. Some better than others." Sigurd blinked and looked up at Regin to accept the offered trencher. "Or so someone told me."

"Some old warrior?" Regin guessed without much interest.

"An old wanderer. Or maybe it was a dream. I'm not sure."

Regin frowned, sensing something but unsure what. "A dream?"

"After Gladung died. He came to me from the woods. Strange woods. And ... there was a sound, a wolf howling."

Regin's frown deepened. "This wanderer—tell me of him."

"I thought he was Odin. But surely not? I think I was sick."

"The Allfather can appear in many forms, some clear, some not. But I would not trust him in any form. You know what they call him?"

"The Betrayer of Warriors, yes," answered Sigurd. "I know the tale of my father's death, how Odin shattered the sword that he himself had given."

"Even that you do not resent?"

"My father was an old man. Odin gave him a battle-death before his glory could wane."

"Hm. The *All*father. The Father of Good—and the Father of Evil."

Sigurd's golden eyebrows pinched. "He said something like that. About working good and evil with one hand. I wish I could remember ..."

"He is ever enigmatic. Shadowy. I know this, for I met him once."

The golden eyebrows jumped. "You did?"

"Long ago. In a story I may tell you one day. But not tonight."

"Regin—"

"I see you did not lose your sword." Regin nodded to the weapon, which Sigurd had brought to the hearth fire, forgetting the bad manners of it.

Sigurd's hand went to the pommel, his fingers brushing the crown of the dragon's head. "This is precious to me."

"May I see it?"

When Sigurd had passed the weapon to him over the fire, Regin examined its edges, which had been dulled and chipped, though its balance remained perfect. "Hjalprek gave this to you."

"How did you know?"

"There is no other way you could have come by it, for I gave it to him."

"You made this sword?"

"Why should that surprise you? I have made many weapons for Danish kings." Regin handed it back. "I will sharpen it tomorrow. It looks like you've been digging with it."

Sigurd sheathed the sword. "Why did you leave the Danish court to farm? There must have been greater honor in being a smith there?"

"Oh, aye. Honor given by another man. Comfort in the shelter and shadow of another man's hall. Here, at least, I am my own man. Kings come to *me*. For my work. For my words." Regin stirred the pot again. "Eat, boy. It's going cold."

Sigurd broke the skin that had formed on his stew and ate a few bites. "Your cook is very good." When Regin raised an eyebrow at this obvious play for information, Sigurd flushed. "It's only that … it's so quiet here. Yet …" Sigurd's eyes went to the loom standing along the wall, warped with wool of the same green as his tunic.

Regin settled himself on his stool, relenting to say, "Lofnheith made the stew. And, yes, my sister is a good cook.

And a fine weaver. But make no mistake: she is quite mad. Stay away from her."

Sigurd lay sleepless in his chamber, buried under sheepskins, suffocated by the stillness of a silent place. Hjalprek's hall had never been silent, never still, even in the dead of night. Always, someone could be heard: snoring, shifting, coupling, shuffling about in the dim hours to bake the bread. Sigurd's nights as he traveled had been livelier yet, the wind teasing at the trees and grasses, the rain dripping. And there had been the animals and insects, always moving, always speaking. Regin's house was like a held breath.

Then, amid that dead silence, Sigurd heard someone humming. It drifted through his door from the hall, high and musical and eerie.

Slipping from the bed, Sigurd crept over the rushes in his bare feet. He eased the door open an inch and pressed his eye to the slit. The hearth yet glowed with coals, creating a faint bloom of light, enough to reveal a woman moving through the hall, her robes a pale smudge in the dimness. As she neared the hearth, her fair hair caught threads of light, and the glow through her gown revealed a thin figure.

"Ghost," she called musically, and the owl let out a soft hu-hu-hu-huhu from the rafters. Lofnheith, for it must be her, hummed again and seemed to gaze into the embers—then she plunged her hands into them.

She scooped up a handful of glowing coals and held them near her face. "I see, I see," she murmured. "I see and remember."

When her eyes jumped to Sigurd, he jerked back, startled. Recovering himself, he opened the door. Lofnheith drifted his way, the burning coals held aloft in her bare hands, ashes spilling down her gown. The embers glowed upon a sharp but striking face, with high cheekbones and a bladelike nose and eyes as dark as a starless night. She had an ageless look, with her ashy-gold hair and smooth, sharp face, but Sigurd knew she must be very, very old.

"Beautiful," she lilted. "So beautiful."

Sigurd was not sure whether to be fascinated or horrified. "What is beautiful—Lofnheith?"

"The wings and the claws and the gold and dying. And the flames, of course, the flames."

Sigurd looked at her fine hands, where the glowing coals were reddening her skin and lighting the tips of her long fingernails. "You will hurt yourself."

Suddenly, Lofnheith let out a bloodcurdling scream and dropped the coals into the rushes. She turned and fled the hall, vanishing into the dimness like a ghost.

Sigurd stared after her—then remembered the coals. He ran to the hearth and snatched up an iron pot and poker. He raced back to where the coals burned among the dry rushes. As he swept them into the pot, Regin emerged from a chamber, drawing his robes tight.

"Regin—your sister—"

Regin stalked over, scowling. "What did she say?"

"She picked up the coals with her bare hands—"

"But what did she *say*?"

"Nothing. Nonsense! Flames, wings, gold—I don't know!"

Regin halted and sighed. "More of the same, then. Never mind."

As Regin turned to go, Sigurd called, "But her hands. She must be burned—"

"Don't worry about her. Dump those coals and go back to bed. I told you: she is mad."

Though Sigurd asked to watch him sharpen the sword, Regin did not allow it. He knew what sometimes happened when he lost himself in his work. He could not always hold his human form.

Even if he could, he would not share his craft. Many young smiths had come to him over the years, begging him to teach them. But the depth of craft their common minds and clumsy hands could learn could be taught by anyone. What he did was beyond them, and it was his alone. He could hear the voice of the metal—he could give it form.

At the edge of the farm, his cave-like smithy lay within a hill, for it was close to the earth that Regin could best understand the language of the ores. Thinly beaten silver mirrors caught the forge's light and cast it onto the rough stone walls, over the anvil and scattered tools. Regin worked at his bench, filing away imperfections, finding the true edges of the sword he had made for Hjalprek so long ago. When the edges were even and sharp, he polished the sword against an oiled whetstone, brightening the swirling, snakelike pattern of light and dark. As he smoothed the blade against the stone, he heard an echo of the frustration he had wrought into it. Listening to the sword now, he was surprised. He must have sensed, even then, that Hjalprek would never be what he needed.

When Regin returned the sword to Sigurd, the boy held it to the sky. Sunlight streamed down the gleaming blade to bathe his face. His blue eyes sparkled like sapphires and his hair shone like gold. "It's beautiful," he said. "Thank you, Regin."

A strange pain twisted through Regin's heart, a pain that a cold, lonely man like Regin could not recognize. So he told himself that it was gold lust, nothing more.

As spring warmed to summer, Regin left Sigurd largely to his own devices. Sigurd fished and hunted in the river valley. He practiced his archery. When he complained of having no opponent for sword practice, Regin met him in the yard with a blade of his own.

Though no swordsman, Regin was stronger than Sigurd and far more cunning. Unlike Hjalprek's thanes, Regin punished mistakes with ruthless blows. He offered little advice, but that suited Sigurd well, for he preferred to find his own way and did not mind the cuts and bruises that were his teachers. His style shifted away from the formal training of the Danish thanes and became a fluid, instinctive thing.

Despite Sigurd's objection, Regin forced him to use a shield sometimes. Only this did he insist on teaching: how to make the shield a weapon, how to turn a block into a blow. Sigurd learned the skills and in his life would use them a handful of times, but never was that his true way. He was only brilliant when he was himself, fearless and moving forward.

Regin also sent him on a number of errands, some of which took several days. He was sent to buy grains, to sell fleece, to cut firewood. Sometimes Regin set a task with no obvious purpose.

"Fill this basket with mud from the bottom of the river," Regin once instructed. "Go out to the middle, where the mud is best."

"Best for what?"

"For the leeks. They need nourishment, to grow above the grass."

At this time, the river was swollen with spring rains, and the cold shot through Sigurd when he dove into it from the bridge. He was blind in the river's murk, buffeted by currents, his lungs burning from lack of air long before he found the bottom. He scraped silt and mud into the basket then fought his way to the surface with the dragging weight. By the time he made it to shore, flopping onto his back in exhaustion with the basket sloshing beside him, he was some distance downstream.

When he reached the bridge, hauling the heavy burden, he found Regin there. The smith gave a subtle smile. "What fine leeks we'll have."

One day in late summer, Sigurd returned from fishing, thumping down a bucket teeming with glistening trout, and said, "I thought you would teach me things."

"I am teaching you things," replied Regin from where he sat on the porch stoop smoothing a spear shaft with shavegrass. "Why? What did you expect?"

Sigurd did not want to admit that he had expected magic and mysteries. He did not want to ask again about the Glittering Heath, as he had one night, only to hear Regin laugh. "This I will say for it," Regin had chuckled, "at least the tales keep cowards away."

So when Regin asked what he had expected, Sigurd only shrugged, and Regin punished the question with a day spent poring over maps, punctuated with a lecture on the fragility of kingdoms. Regin talked about power: who lost it, who gained it, and why. Sigurd, chin resting on his folded arms, listened without interest.

"This"—Regin stabbed a finger at a spot by Sigurd's elbow, making him lurch up from his slouch—"is Burgundy, kingdom of the Nibelungs. Its king, Gjuki, lacks the heavy army of his eastern neighbor Budli of Hunaheim"—now Regin pointed to a kingdom separated from Gjuki's by a dense forest—"but Gjuki has the Rhine, and better trade." Regin frowned at Sigurd's glazed eyes, like water scummed by stillness. "You don't even know where we are on the map, do you?"

Sigurd traced his finger along the Rhine to the tributary that was Regin's river valley and stopped on almost the right spot. "Here?"

It surprised Regin. He needed to remember this: that Sigurd was not stupid, and even when he appeared to be woolgathering, he might not be.

Regin nudged Sigurd's finger a few miles west. "Here."

Then Sigurd dragged his finger northward to an unmarked section of the map, halting in the heart of the Glittering Heath. A chill raced up Regin's spine.

"What is here?" Sigurd asked.

The boy had asked about the Heath before. Did he know he was pointing at it? Should Regin speak of it? But it was too soon—surely, it was too soon? So he only said, "Don't worry about that," and flicked Sigurd's finger away from it. "But here"—Regin stabbed at Burgundy again—"consider the Darkwood between Burgundy and Hunaheim. It shapes all conflicts between them. Is it protection or danger?"

"I would think it hard to bring an army through it."

"Aye." Regin warmed to the topic again. He loved strategy. "But easy to hide one."

Sigurd leaned on his elbow with a sigh. "I suppose so."

"Am I boring you, son of Sigmund?"

Sigurd straightened at the warning tone. "No, Regin."

"You do not lie well, Sigurd. You should avoid it whenever possible. I am dismayed, though, to find you so uninterested in the kingdom of your foster brother." At Sigurd's blank stare, Regin smiled, pleased that Ælf's coldness with the boy had made him withhold what would have been welcome information. Now, it was Regin's gift to give, for though Sigurd plainly liked his own company, it was obvious that he was growing bored with the quiet, solitary life of the river valley. Regin said, "Gunnar is about your age, and King Gjuki's oldest son."

Sigurd perked up. "He is coming here?"

Regin smiled wolfishly. "I leave tomorrow for Burgundy. I suppose we shall see."

82

Of Lofnheith, Sigurd had seen little since that first night when she held burning embers in her bare hands and spoke so strangely. Though he knew she kept the house, she seemed to move in and out of the shadows like a ghost, and he caught only fleeting glimpses of her.

But one night after Regin had gone, Sigurd was hauling his evening's catch up the slope from the river when he caught sight of Lofnheith at the top. From Sigurd's angle, she reared tall against the red-tinged sky, like a carven pillar of a goddess. So wraithlike did she always seem that Sigurd half expected her to fade into the air, but she was still there when he reached the top.

Sigurd followed her gaze north across the dusky hills. "What are you looking at, Lofnheith?"

Her white gown drifted in tatters around her ankles, and her feet were bare in the grass. Her ashy hair hung limp about her shoulders. She spoke as though in a trance. "Three times they burned me. Witch they called me, but speak they bid me, from death and darkness. Of their doom I told, and their deserving. They did not like what I saw."

At this dark speech, Sigurd's skin tightened with gooseflesh. "Who burned you?"

Lofnheith clutched suddenly at her breast and cried out as though wounded. She fell into Sigurd, gripping his shoulder to catch herself. Her hand was as hard and fierce as a claw, her fingernails like talons. Startled to be touched by her, Sigurd recoiled slightly, but he did not pull away; she would have fallen.

"Lofnheith—"

Her eyes squeezed shut. "Poor boy, kin of my kin, kin of the evil one, all unknowing, born for so many revenges. How I hate you. How I love you." Tears leaked from her closed eyes, spilling down her ageless cheeks to the sharp line of her jaw. She released Sigurd suddenly and stood straight as a carven pillar again, a hand up to silence him, though he had not spoken. Her eyes had flown open. "Do you hear him?"

Sigurd frowned. "I hear only the wind and the river."

"Across the Heath he flies, roaring his terror and his beauty."

Sigurd's skin tightened once more. "The Heath?"

"Shined and fined, it glitters like stars under his wings."

A thrill shot through Sigurd. Regin had brushed his questions away like mere sawdust, but here was another who might know, and he had not thought to ask her. "The Glittering Heath? What flies over it? Lofnheith, tell me—what haunts the Heath?"

"Speak they bid me, speak and burn. But in what fire? There are so many. All killing one thing to birth another. He flies between the stars above and stars below—but no. Not tonight. *Then*. And *then*." Her eyes squeezed shut again and fresh tears spilled down her cheeks. "Threefold my mind, threefold the time—do I spin or measure or cut?"

Sigurd shivered. Mad she might be, but her words weighed upon him, like truths too dark and terrible to understand.

Lofnheith's thin shoulders caved in, and she looked suddenly more like a woman, fragile and forlorn, than she ever had. She gazed upon the bucket of fish that Sigurd was yet holding, which he had all but forgotten.

"Such lies they tell, that he ate his fish with eyes closed because he could not bear to see it diminish. But that is *their* greed speaking, for greed is all they understand. Otter was a simple creature, who closed his eyes in simple pleasure. Murder most foul did they two commit, three eyes upon the deed, though one hand threw the stone."

Sigurd's head spun. She spoke in such riddles. But there was little good in questioning her, and she was shivering, so Sigurd took her hand, ignoring the prick of her awful fingernails. "Come," he said, "let us go inside."

They sat together at the hearth that night, the white-faced owl silent above them. The night was warm, but still Lofnheith shivered, so Sigurd draped a blanket around her shoulders and handed her a trencher of fish soup. She reached out a hand from the folds of cloth and stroked his hair as a grandmother might.

"He works his will on all of us. You, too, will learn to hate him."

"Who?" asked Sigurd, and the owl echoed softly, "Hu-hu-hu?" but there was no answer, for Lofnheith was staring into the fire with dread and a strange sort of longing.

Chapter Seven

N OT UNTIL THE CORN Cutting Month did Regin return, and he returned alone. By this time, Sigurd, who had no interest in the dull, repetitive work of harvest, had taken to collecting herbs with Lofnheith—when he could find her, for she still came and went in her uncanny way. But more and more he did find her, for she let him.

She taught him nothing directly, but she demonstrated much wisdom: she knew which mushrooms to cut, knew how to find wild honey, knew when the weather was changing. Sometimes she petted Sigurd's hair as she had that night by the hearth, and he found he did not mind this.

One day, a blue tit alighted on a branch nearby and let out a rolling trill. Lofnheith nodded as though a person had spoken. Then she looked at Sigurd with rare and present clarity and said, "You must learn the speech of birds, grandson. It will save your life, once."

The way she addressed him, as though they were kin, he regarded as perhaps affectionate but more likely meaningless, for he was not sure she even knew his name. Still, he shivered at the chill of her fateful words. Amid her mutterings, there was truth; he was sure of it.

On the day the blue tit trilled, they were up in the high meadow, and Lofnheith pointed to the valley below. Though empty at the time, a little while later Regin appeared in that very spot, a solitary dark figure on a dark horse.

By the time Regin dismounted in the yard, Sigurd was there to meet him. "What of Gunnar?" he asked, even as Regin's foot touched the ground.

Regin, who cared little for courtesy himself, did not rebuke the rude impatience but only untied his saddlebags. "He won't take as long as you did. He doesn't have nearly as far to travel. If he makes it."

Sigurd was aghast. "He is a king's son."

Regin lifted a wry, dark eyebrow. "So are you."

"But my father is dead. Are you not worried how Gjuki might respond—"

"If I am worried, it is my worry and not yours."

Gunnar arrived a week later, while Sigurd and Regin were engrossed in sword practice in the yard. Sigurd made a stab at Regin's torso, but Regin knocked the thrust aside with his greater strength and returned heavy blows. Sigurd dodged the first and caught the second against his cross-guard. As he tried to twist Regin's sword from his grip, Regin kicked him in the chest, making Sigurd stagger back. Regin brought down his sword to end the fight, but Sigurd caught the blow against his cross-guard again and this time he got the twist right. Regin's sword spun from his grasp.

A look of surprise flashed across Regin's face. When Sigurd began to lower his sword, thinking the match won, Regin kicked Sigurd's feet out from under him and pinned him to the ground, pressing a knife to Sigurd's throat.

Anger flashed across Sigurd's face. "But that's cheating! You said swords *only*!"

"And did you learn your lesson?"

"That people *lie*?"

Regin grinned wolfishly, enjoying the boy's rare display of temper. "If you like. Or expect the unexpected. Prepare for everything."

Sigurd's retort was cut off by an exclamation from across the yard. "A superb exhibition!"

Gunnar of Burgundy leapt down from his chestnut stallion. Though of an age with Sigurd, his round face and shorter, stockier build made him look younger. He had a proud bearing, and though he was smiling, there was a determined, conscious set to his mouth. His dark hair, as dark as Regin's, was combed back neatly. He wore the fine clothes of a king's son, gold-embroidered and well-fitted. His belts and trappings displayed elaborate tooling. Behind him, two men, nobles by their own dress, were dismounting.

Sigurd scrambled to his feet as Regin let out a piercing whistle that brought Hama from the dairy to take the horses. Bending to retrieve his lost sword, Regin said, "Arrived safely I see, Gunnar."

Gunnar gave him a peevish look. "Thanks to the escort of my cousins, yes." Gunnar formally introduced the two men, who nodded stiffly, then he turned to Sigurd with an air of excitement. "Your kin are held in high esteem in my father's kingdom. I shall be proud to claim Sigurd the Volsung as my brother, for brothers is what we shall be, even unto death."

Gunnar's face was so earnest and his presence so welcome that Sigurd found himself smiling in spite of the grandiose speech, a thing he usually detested. Clasping Gunnar's offered forearm, he said, "I never had any brothers."

Gunnar grinned and looked like he would speak again, but Regin interrupted. "Come, boys. Everyone will want to wash before supper."

As they sat around the low-burning hearth fire for the evening meal, Gunnar told of his travels: of the weather, of a merchant charging obscene rates for simple cooking ware, of the night his stallion broke its tether and took all the next day to find. He left out any reference to Regin having abandoned him on the road, and Regin certainly said nothing of it. Gunnar's cousins gave no indication that they knew what had happened. It was not until two days later, after the men had departed for Burgundy, that Regin spoke of it.

He had brought files and whetstones from his smithy, and they sat in the cool of the hall at a sturdy oak table. Though Regin would not teach his craft of making, he condescended to guide the boys through the proper sharpening of their swords, spearheads and knives. They were both, he said, terrible at it. It was hard to teach without demonstrating, but Regin would not wield the tools himself. He had once in front of Sigurd, and he still wondered what the boy had seen. Sigurd hoarded his thoughts like a dragon.

Wiping excess oil from a whetstone, Regin handed it to Gunnar and said, "You did not tell your kinsmen of my mean trick."

Gunnar lifted his chin. "It was a matter between you and me—and no concern of theirs."

"Is that so?"

"A king must have discretion," Gunnar explained. "He must know what to tell his people and what to keep to himself. It would only have caused trouble, for they would have reported it to my father, and he might have been pressured to revoke my fosterage. Perhaps you did not realize this, but you left me not five miles from their lands."

"So what did you tell them?"

"Only that I needed an escort. They thought you rude, of course, but assumed you had intended for me to come to them. If you think me cowardly for not riding on alone"—Gunnar's voice rose—"I will remind you that I am my father's heir, and it would be nothing short of stupid for me to risk my life on perilous roads, for nothing."

"Of course," Regin agreed.

"It would be irresponsible. I have more to think of than myself."

"Naturally."

"I would gladly risk—even yield—my life for a worthy cause, one that serves my father's kingdom, but foolish risks are only that: foolish."

"I see you understand a little of what it means to be king. That is not without value. But, Gunnar, you may have other things to learn, things less comfortable to you. I hope I will not find you unwilling."

"Of course not," objected Gunnar. "That is why I am here. It is my duty to bring some greater renown to my people." This seeming to be his final point, Gunnar turned his attention to his sword, running his finger along the edge to test its smoothness. Then he looked up at Sigurd. "Did he leave you on the road?"

"Yes."

"And what did you do?"

"I rode here alone." Sigurd's face heated. "Foolishly, I suppose." Only in hearing Gunnar's account did Sigurd realize he could have handled his situation differently. It had not occurred to him to seek help.

Gunnar gaped at him. "But it must have taken weeks! All the way from *Denmark*? Did you meet trouble?"

Sigurd stroked the whetstone evenly against his sword, concentrating on the angle as Regin had instructed. "My horse was killed. A man tried to rob me."

"A man killed your horse and tried to rob you?"

Sigurd floundered. They were separate events, with much before and after each, but he did not want to speak of the outlaws who had taken him captive. He did not like to think about that time.

"My horse fell," said Sigurd, but the lie weighed on him, for it took from Gladung the honor of his death, so he amended, "He fell while saving my life."

"From the man who tried to rob you?"

Sigurd had actually been referring to the would-be thief he had killed later, south of the Elbe, but it was not much of a lie, for the outlaws he had fled had indeed robbed him, so he said only, "Mm."

Regin's icy blue eyes narrowed. "A few months here and you've forgotten how to speak for yourself? The boy I met in the Danish hall was not so meek. You would kill this man, I hope, if you saw him again."

"I did kill him," Sigurd replied sharply. "Well—that one." He shook his head. "Fine. Here is what happened: two men captured me one night, not long after you left me. I escaped, but they shot my horse. He ran as far as he could then fell, and so he died. Later, a *different* man tried to rob me. Him, I killed. Then I came here. That is all."

"That is *all?*" echoed Gunnar. "There are *hours* of story in that. And a song, I should think! I could write up a few lines ..." Gunnar trailed off at Sigurd's frown. "Well, why not? You should be proud."

"I am proud."

Now it was Gunnar who frowned. "But ..."

"I just—I don't like talking about myself. It makes things feel ... smaller. Less real maybe. I prefer to just know things for myself."

Gunnar's frown of confusion deepened, but a thoughtful look came into Regin's eyes.

In the first days of Gunnar's fosterage, Sigurd would often disappear as he was used to doing, not to be seen again until the afternoon, when he might return with a brace of summer-fat hares or a bucket of fish. Gunnar was not used to the tedious solitude this forced upon him, and he was certainly not used to being avoided. And so he caught up with Sigurd in the stable one morning to, as he described it, "deal with this."

"I'm not avoiding you," Sigurd protested, startled by the accusation. No one had ever cared before whether he came or went.

Gunnar's eyes hardened. "If you prefer your own company to mine—fine. Keep it." He turned to leave.

Sigurd did not understand Gunnar's anger, but he did see that he was about to lose something, so he called after him, "Wait. Don't go."

Gunnar turned back, but his chin was lifted defiantly. When Sigurd only stood there, unsure what to do next, Gunnar's expression softened. "Do you have *any* friends?"

"No." Regin's black gelding nosed at Sigurd's back, sniffing for grain. Sigurd resisted the urge to pet the animal. Gunnar had not meant equine friends.

Gunnar winced. "I didn't mean that like it sounded."

"It sounded like a question, so I answered it."

Gunnar blinked in surprise at the bluntness.

"Um ..." Sigurd shifted, suddenly awkward and acutely aware of the horse now hanging its head over his shoulder. "Do you want to come with me? It might be boring," he added hastily. That was what boys his age usually told him, that he was boring. But then, he found *them* boring.

Some of the peevishness returned to Gunnar's expression. "It's boring *here*."

"Well ... I want to check my snares. Then maybe we could make some new targets for spear practice?"

At Gunnar's relieved, "By Odin, yes," Sigurd smiled and felt a strange sensation in his chest, like something had opened.

Sigurd could not entirely cease his solitary wanderings, and sometimes after that he would still vanish for a day, but Gunnar began to treat his disappearances as a matter of course. "Back from the dead?" he would tease upon Sigurd's return, and Sigurd learned to tease back. "Did you mourn me? Were you lonely?" Gunnar would roll his eyes or poke him or sometimes simply say, "Yes." As for weapons practice, that also took some adjustment on both sides.

"By the gods!" Gunnar exclaimed during one of their first sessions, swiping at his bloodied nose after Sigurd had cracked an elbow into it. "Is this how you spar?"

Sigurd lowered his sword. "Regin and I always spar this way."

Blood dripped onto Gunnar's embroidered blue tunic. "That is *absurd*. He's twice your size."

"No, he's not, and I'm certainly not twice *your* size."

Gunnar reddened. "Well, I wasn't expecting—" He gestured vaguely in Sigurd's direction. "—*that*."

"That *what*?"

"*You*, Volsung, you ridiculous brute."

Sigurd laughed, delighted by that. Gunnar glared for a moment, then a smile broke across his bloodied face. "I'm sorry I hit you," said Sigurd. "I get caught up in it."

"I suppose I should expect no less from—"

Sigurd grinned. "A ridiculous brute?"

"A *Volsung*. The least you can do is show me how you did that."

Sigurd tried, but his instructions amounted to "you just feel it" and "you sense where your opponent is going to step."

95

Gunnar would give him an incredulous look or simply sigh and say, "Show me again."

On a day they played at mounted archery, Sigurd rode Regin's placid black gelding, for the heavy roan he had ridden here was even more sluggish. There was no question that Gunnar's was the finer horse, as fine, perhaps, as Gladung. The chestnut stallion was heavily muscled but light-footed, highly trained. After a few passes by the targets, Gunnar offered Raudfaxi for Sigurd to ride.

At Sigurd's protest, Gunnar only shrugged. "You're clearly the better rider."

Sigurd leaped into Raudfaxi's saddle and kicked the stallion into a gallop. They flew across the field until Sigurd brought the horse to a sliding stop. Wheeling Raudfaxi on his haunches, Sigurd came racing back, hollering with joy.

Astride Regin's horse, Gunnar snorted. "Dreadful showoff."

They galloped past their painted targets, loosing arrows with shouts and laughter. When Gunnar sent an arrow sailing into the red heart of a target, Sigurd exclaimed, "You're very good!"

Gunnar gave him a haughty grin. "Don't look so surprised, Volsung."

They spent time, too, in study. Regin spoke of strategy: in war, in alliances, in law-making. Gunnar would listen and argue, his whole body leaning into the conversation. One day, Regin brought a sack of stones and iron slag from his smithy. He swept the rushes from the floor and arranged the stones and slag to represent the ranks of two opposing armies. He made mountains of woven baskets, rivers of narrow cloth, forests of scattered grain. One army he gave to Gunnar, another to Sigurd. He weighted the odds unevenly, a difference in numbers, an advantage of terrain.

As the boys moved their bands of warriors, Regin would demand their reasons. What would this move achieve? What results did they expect?

Gunnar complained, exasperated, "If I have to explain myself, Sigurd will know my plans, and they'll be ruined."

"Your point is well taken," said Regin. He had been waiting for one of them to address this problem, to think of secrets. He was not surprised it was Gunnar—and he was not surprised by Sigurd's obvious disinterest.

When he pressed Sigurd on this, the boy said, "I do not see the point. Men are not stones to be moved about. A band of warriors is not a lump of slag to compare in size to another lump of slag. This game takes no account of *will*. It takes no account of the skills or the hearts of the men who are fighting. And in any case—is this what matters? Is this what the gods weigh?"

"It is what a king weighs," said Gunnar.

Sigurd sighed.

He was far happier when he and Gunnar worked their weapons in the yard or hunted the woods of the river valley, harvesting deer and foxes for meat and fur. As autumn deepened, they did much of this, for Regin was busy. Several commissions had come in, two from wealthy chieftains—and one from King Budli of Hunaheim.

"The sword is to be a gift from King Budli to his son Atli," Budli's envoy announced after draining a cup of mead. "King Budli is certain of Atli's great destiny to conquer and rule—"

He made a sweeping gesture as though to encompass the world, and his eyes slipped to Gunnar. "—and he would have his son's might sharpened by the finest blade money can buy."

Regin frowned into his own cup. He did not appreciate the tone of command and was tempted to refuse outright. He was no man's subject and would work as he chose. Controlling the impulse, he hedged, "Money can only buy so much. Besides, Gunnar, son of King Gjuki of Burgundy, is my foster son. What manner of blade should I forge for his father's former enemy?"

The envoy swatted this away. "The Budlungs and Nibelungs have been at peace these twenty years. There's no need to dwell on past troubles."

"So you say," Gunnar broke in, his knuckles white on his mead horn. "But what of the reparations yet owed to Burgundy for the burning of field and fold? Where is the respect of the Budlungs for the Nibelungs when such remains unpaid?"

Color flooded the envoy's meaty face above his braided beard. "Those reparations were demanded by the Nibelungs but never agreed upon by the Budlungs. There is no debt owed!"

"Peace, Gunnar," Regin warned as Gunnar's face twisted furiously. "What would your father think of you stirring up trouble with your hotheaded words?"

In the end, Regin agreed to make the sword. To refuse might shatter the uneasy peace between Gunnar's father and King Budli, and it was too soon for that. In addition to the commissioned sword, he planned a letter and a gold torque for Gjuki, keen to avoid a misunderstanding that might jeopardize his fosterage of Gunnar. The boy might lack Sigurd's qualities, but he had others, ones that Sigurd needed. Such opposites they were, yet somehow ... they fit—like a single, completed thing.

As the days darkened toward winter, a plume of smoke slipped continually from the mouth of Regin's smithy, rising through the bare branches of the surrounding trees to disappear on the wind. Within, Regin held black rods of niello in the brazier's shivering light, fingered copper wire and glittering gems, considered the lusters of brass and bronze. He hated laboring for men, but he loved his craft. It was in his nature.

As he lost himself in the work, he shrank and shriveled into his truth and the forge fire cast his hunched shadow upon the wall. His fingers lengthened and grew as knobby as twigs upon the metals. Bastard, his father had called him, and he was. There had been no hiding that at his birth.

One day, as he worked the bellows, the fire blazing intermittently against his craggy face, he paused, listening. From the house drifted the faint notes of Gunnar's harp. When Gunnar had first brought forth his harp after his arrival, Regin had felt a pang of regret. Gunnar had a fine voice and nimble fingers. He could have learned much of the craft, had the skald's path been his. Perhaps, though, the talent would serve him someday, even as a king or warrior. Regin lacked the true foresight to know such a thing. Lofnheith was the one with that gift.

Chapter Eight

IN GENERATIONS PAST, merchants, traders, even whole bands of warriors would disappear from the Rhine where it passed near the Glittering Heath—but that was long ago and few now remembered that terrible history, or that once a fine city had thrived at the Heath's edge, on the banks of a tributary, under the towering hills. The Heath had lain quiet for long and long, and only those who dwelled near remembered to fear it; but even their fears, passed down too many times, were shadowy, shapeless things. Only a few knew anything of the truth. One of those few was King Gjuki of Burgundy.

Memory is long where wrong is done, and so the Nibelungs remembered that place. That memory was the property of the king and also his burden, which he passed to his heir as soon as possible—for with it went the duty to avenge an old wrong.

Gunnar already bore the weight of this duty, pressed upon him by his father with relief, but he did not understand what that duty required of him. His father had been unclear, as Gjuki's own father had been. Still, Gunnar felt keenly the weight of his father's expectation, of his family's long-buried shame. It was that which led him to sneak into Regin's room one day while Sigurd was wandering the icy river valley and the smith was busy with his work.

An odd room it was, the cluttered opposite of the sparse hall, with cushions and blankets and sheepskins, stacks of vellum maps and other writings, wax tablets and quills and pots of ink. The busyness reminded Gunnar of his mother's private room, though he had only glimpsed it on one occasion—and she had quickly shut the door in his face. This room, though, did not smell strange and bitter, as hers had. This room smelled of dust, which fuzzed every surface.

Among Regin's more mundane possessions lay scattered trinkets. Not trinkets though: gold and silver, amber and pearl. Such wealth, yet Regin displayed none of it on his dark, plain clothing. Some of the treasures looked very old, some quite foreign. Gunnar did not know what the Nibelung hoard would look like, how it would be different from any other treasure, but nothing here called to him. Would it? How many generations had passed since the wealth of his people had been stolen?

At the sound of shuffling, Gunnar spun—then froze at the sight of Lofnheith's ghostly form in the doorway: feet bare in the rushes, ashy hair drifting like cobweb, white gown hanging in tatters. In an otherwise empty face her dark eyes reflected firelight, though there was none to reflect.

"He surrounds it all with his arms," she sang out in a breathy voice.

It took Gunnar some moments to find his tongue. "Regin? Or …" The other name froze in his mouth. "Surrounds what?"

"Threefold my mind, threefold the time, but that is always true. No——" Her dark eyes widened, and the fire they held blazed fiercely, then died. "Not always. Death. One curse lifted. Another cast in a shower of gold."

"A shower of gold——"

"Ashes. All ashes, whipped away on the wind. All burned. All gone."

"Gold does not burn."

Tears spilled from Lofnheith's dark eyes down to her sharp jaw. "Men burn. With greed and hate—they burn and burn and burn and burn."

"But the gold——"

"He surrounds it all with his arms."

"You speak of …"

"Or does he drag himself across the Heath, shining and fining it? Does he sleep? Does he wake? Threefold my mind——"

"Lofnheith, tell me of him, tell me of …" He forced the name out: "Fafnir."

She shuddered so hard it seemed she would fall, then she hugged herself, hunching like an old woman. "Speak they bid me, from death and darkness. Of their doom I told, and their deserving. They did not like what I saw."

"Lofnheith, whose——"

Gunnar blinked. She was gone, like a misty apparition. From the rafters of the hall, the owl called softly hu-hu-huuuh.

As winter melted away, the ewes dropped their lambs and the shearing was done. Feet deep in the spring mud, Sigurd and Gunnar helped with this hard and dirty work, for they could not be spared from it. When Sigurd asked Gunnar what troubled him, for his friend's mouth had been grimly set for weeks, Gunnar said, "Shameful labor, this, for the sons of kings. Even Regin does not lower himself to it."

Sigurd did not mind the work and said so. Gunnar turned away and spoke no more. Not long after, Gunnar vanished during the night from his place by the hearth, where he and Sigurd had been sleeping for warmth in spring's lingering chill. Some instinct woke Sigurd, or perhaps the owl's restless hooting. He felt at once that he was alone, even before his eyes fell upon the depression in the rushes where Gunnar's bedroll had been.

When he found Gunnar's bedroom empty and his weapons gone, a memory pressed forward in Sigurd's mind. "What side is Lofnheith on?" Gunnar had muttered the other day as she drifted from the hall. When Sigurd had echoed, "Side?" Gunnar had started, as though he had not meant to speak aloud.

Sigurd snatched up his sword, stuffed a pouch with dried meat and bread, grabbed his waterskin, then went out to the stable, surprised to find Raudfaxi in his stall. At a loss, he walked across the yard and looked north, as he often did. Movement caught his eye. The moon was up, bright and full-bellied, or he would not have seen the figure on the other side of the river, where lay the remains of an old road.

Sigurd had followed this road before, riding an hour or two through grassy fields and along thickets beyond the river valley, where the gravel was worn almost to nothing in places. He thought often of this faded path, which cut north toward that blank spot on the map that Regin would not explain.

Trailing at a distance, Sigurd did not make himself known to Gunnar until the sky was lightening. By this time, he had seen what—or rather, whom—Gunnar was following. Far ahead, Lofnheith had stopped to rest, and Gunnar had settled on the barely visible remains of the old road, his bow ready beside him. Sigurd had been moving through a thicket skirting the road's eastern edge, keeping out of sight.

"Gunnar!" he whisper-shouted, and Gunnar sprang to his feet, his bow swinging Sigurd's way. Sigurd ducked behind a tree, not trusting twitchy fingers on a bowstring. "It's Sigurd," he announced and stepped slowly into view, shocked to find Gunnar's arrow yet trained upon him.

Gunnar's eyes narrowed. "Why are you following me?"

"Because you left so strangely. Why are *you* following Lofnheith?"

The bow lowered, Gunnar's pull easing, but he did not lay the weapon down. His brown eyes were cold and hard. "It's no concern of yours, Volsung."

"Then perhaps I should ask Lofnheith," Sigurd said, stung.

"You would take *her* side?"

"You keep speaking of sides. Why?"

"It's no con—"

Sigurd cut in before Gunnar could repeat his offensive words. "She's heading toward the Glittering Heath." When Gunnar blanched, Sigurd stepped forward, pressing, "You know this, and you know something is there. Regin would not speak of it. Lofnheith spoke unclearly. Tell me."

"She spoke of it to you?"

"Lay down your bow." Only when Gunnar did so, did Sigurd speak again. "She is troubled. Someone hurt her—"

"Do not pity her. She is part of it."

"Part of *what?*" Sigurd came to meet Gunnar on the faded swath of gravel.

"It is a family matter. I cannot speak of it to—"

"A mere foster brother?"

Color stained Gunnar's round cheeks. "It's not that simple. My father spoke to me in confidence. Even Hogni, my own birth brother, doesn't know. How, then, could I tell another, *any* other? Not that I know much. That is why I must follow her. She's part of it. She knows something."

"What lies on the Heath? Lofnheith spoke of something flying over it. I thought she was talking about a bird but—"

"Not a bird. Certainly not a bird."

Gooseflesh tightened Sigurd's skin. "What, then?"

"Something terrible. I don't know."

"But you know something. You say it's no concern of mine, but I am here too, fostered with Regin as you are, our fate threads twined together. There must be purpose to that. And you were right when you said I know little of friends and brothers, but I know enough not to let one take a dangerous road alone."

"And you're curious."

"Aye," Sigurd admitted with a slight smile. "That too. Ever since I first heard tales of the Heath. I would have traveled this road eventually."

"Out of mere curiosity?"

"Wouldn't you? It is a great mystery."

"You're a strange one, Volsung."

"It doesn't seem so to me, but others say it often enough. Perhaps it is true."

Gunnar searched Sigurd's face briefly then all the fight went out of him with a sigh. His shoulders slumped. "My family ... By Tyr's right hand, my father would be so angry if he knew I was speaking of this—"

"I will keep your secret."

"Better, I hope, than I am doing."

"Certainly." Gunnar reddened at this. "It is your own secret, so you have the choice to share it or not," Sigurd declared. "It is not mine, and so I have no such choice, and so I will speak of it to no one."

"Upon your life you swear it?"

"Upon my life I swear it."

Gunnar dropped onto his rolled-up bedroll, where he had been sitting when Sigurd first came upon him. For a time, he sat in thought, Sigurd beside him, and worried a thread of blue wool from his cloak, unraveling it from the weaving.

"Once," Gunnar began at last, "long ago, my people had a treasure hoard the likes of which has never since been seen. But that treasure was stolen—by Loki, though I do not know how or why. Perhaps the god of chaos needs no reason for his malice. What I do know is that Loki gave the treasure to a king called Hreidmar. Hreidmar ruled in that day from a great city at the Heath's edge. He is long dead, but his children yet live, for they descend from the race of giants."

When Gunnar fell silent, Sigurd said, "You speak of Lofnheith. And Regin."

"And another. Fafnir. It is he who haunts the Heath and he who holds the hoard."

"And you want it back," Sigurd surmised. "The treasure hoard. That's what this is all about? Following Lofnheith. You, being at Regin's to begin with."

"It belongs to my family by right," Gunnar said stiffly.

"And you think Lofnheith will lead you to it?"

"I suspect the road alone could do that. But I would see what part she plays in this."

Sigurd frowned. "I do not see malice in her."

"And yet she walks this road—and Regin lives near it."

Sigurd's frown deepened. "But what of this other—Fafnir? You said he holds the treasure. What manner of man is he … if he is that at all?"

"I do not know."

"Then we will find out." Sigurd stood and squinted ahead. "Lofnheith is moving. Come, Gunnar. Let us do this."

For a moment, Gunnar looked torn. Then he sighed once more and smiled a little. "Aye, Volsung, for it seems the gods will it so."

Lofnheith searched for the thoughts of birds, but the farther north she walked, the fewer she found. In the silence of their absence, she remembered how lonely life could be. She wept as she walked, weighted down by the ruthless, endless, circular churn of time. She wept as she had when her father demanded the impossible, cursing her when she refused. She wept for the boys following her, though she knew not where she was in time or where they were. She could not tell the visions apart.

Fire and blood, gold and ash, scales of fish and fiend. An endless flow of water. A sword with all the ugly might of men and gods. A boy, a man, a death. But which? Whose? When?

She knew she was mad.

And she knew she was right.

Grassland gave way to a stretch of spring-soggy heath that looked like any other: flat, spotted with low plants, spiky with stiff grasses. But as the sun crossed the sky, the plants grew fewer, the grasses sparser. The soil thinned until only scrub could cling to it, then nothing at all. Where the sun laid bare the rocky ground, it glinted like polished stone.

Rocky hills rose in the distance. They rose to the west as well, where they edged the Rhine. Scraggly, skeletal trees emerged to the east. Late in the day, these features began to converge; the Heath narrowed. Yet on and on walked Lofnheith, tireless, until Sigurd and Gunnar lost sight of her. Between one blink and the next, the white smudge of her was gone. But there was the road to follow, difficult though it was to discern the faded gravel from the other stones. As the day dimmed, this became impossible.

"We should stop," said Gunnar. "We'll lose the path." All his grand boldness seemed to have been worn away; now he was only tired and hungry. Besides, he did not like the look of those rocky hills looming higher and steeper in the distance.

Sigurd pointed ahead. "Look. Do you see? The road is paved up there. And surely that rock face is our destination."

After the sun set blood red and the sky darkened, what had merely glinted across the Heath during the day glittered and gleamed in the moonlight. Sigurd murmured, "It glitters like the stars under his wings."

"What?" Gunnar's heart leaped into his throat. His eyes raced across the sky, but he found only pricks of starlight and the cold moon. "What are you talking about?"

"It's something Lofnheith said. I couldn't remember her exact words until now. But seeing this ... I understand. I can imagine it."

"Imagine *what?*"

The moon shone bright and eerie upon Sigurd's face. "There was a night she picked up glowing coals from the hearth. She held them in her hands, and they did not burn her. Gunnar—I think I know what Fafnir is."

Shoulders hunching, Gunnar silently begged that Sigurd would not say it.

They walked the paved road now. In places, the Heath had swallowed it, then it would emerge, smooth and fine, under their feet. The cliff face reared higher, bleached with moonlight, and humps of stone could be seen to hug its base. Before it all, reflecting the moon, lay a shining ribbon of water.

By the time they reached the riverbank, the stones below the towering cliff revealed their truth: a tumbled city, dead and ruined, nothing now but heaps of shattered stone and the occasional corner of a building to speak of what once had been. Near now, the cliff, which had seemed a sheer face of rock, showed its rough edges. It looked cleaved, as though a giant's axe had harvested its stone and left the rocky innards of the hill exposed and flattened.

Sigurd's gaze was rapt. "I saw such a thing once, though I thought it a fever dream. Through the woods I glimpsed a great stretch of wall, impossibly vast."

Gunnar stood well back from the silvery water, out of the mud and its sparse grass. "What could do such a thing?"

Sigurd looked at Gunnar in surprise. "You said yourself that Regin's kin was of the race of giants. And it was one such who built the great wall of Asgard."

"You cannot be saying you saw the home of the gods."

Sigurd shrugged. "Dreamed it maybe."

"This is no dream, Sigurd, but a fell place. What could destroy a city of stone? And that dark spot in the cliff, where the moonlight disappears ..." Halfway up the cliff face, a mouth of black gaped wide.

"A doorway. See how there is a cut of stone angling up to it?" Sigurd turned his gaze to the river, its surface shining silver, its depths dark and unknown. "I see neither bridge nor boat. We'll have to swim."

"*Swim?*"

As Sigurd unbuckled his sword belt and shrugged off his cloak, Gunnar realized that Sigurd would cross alone. For one moment, Gunnar knew the truth: he himself would not. It was a terrible truth, too sharp, too shaming, so he drove it deep into the darkest corner of himself and said, "Aye, we'll have to swim."

Stripped to their waists, they waded into the river with their shoes, tunics, and weapons bundled into their cloaks and held aloft. Their skin tightened against the cold. When the bottom dropped, the current seized them in a ruthless grip. Gunnar had swum all his life, besting others in contests in the great Rhine, grinning with pride at his strength, but here he flailed and soon lost his bundled weapons and clothes. The river bled the warmth from his blood.

When he went under, he kicked and pulled with all his might. He fought his way up. One gasp, one moment more of air, was all he could win. He sank into the water's cold, dark embrace.

When Sigurd's toes found the mud of the far bank, he looked back and cried out at the sight of empty water. He flung his bundle onto the shore then surged back into the current. Diving under the silvery surface, he pawed and clawed through the dark water, frantic with the impossibility of his search. He broke the surface, gasping for air, then plunged again into the icy murk. Infinite darkness and terrible cold surrounded him. Then, amid the churning black, a light appeared. Silvery and quick, it swept below him, sinuous as a fish, and laughter trilled in his ears, clear and tinkling despite the water's swollen weight.

The light flitted closer, revealing a great silvery tail winding through the dark and a stream of golden hair, softly glowing.

A pair of fine female arms slipped through the currents, twining and twisting until the figure turned over with a flash of small, round breasts. The laughter trilled out again, then the creature swam up to Sigurd, her face, lit with ethereal beauty, drawing itself from the murk. She gazed with large green eyes, shimmering with light, and reached out with a delicate hand to touch Sigurd's cheek.

"Pretty," she burbled, flashing small, pointed teeth. "I could keep you in a box, in a chest, in a trove. How fine your bones would be among the reeds, how bright your eyes would shine amid the pearls, how I would love you, pretty one. Would you love me, too?"

Her small breasts seemed bathed in moonlight, lovely swells, the nipples fine and pink. Her plump lips curved in a smile, and she leaned near, pressing them, cool and soft, to Sigurd's. She seemed to breathe into him, and his body warmed and wakened. She twined her arms with his and wrapped her tail about him. Her breasts pushed into his chest, making him gasp against her plump mouth. Her hair swirled around them both, like a net of finest gold.

Her laughter bubbled out again. "Treasure I find and treasure I keep, sacred and safe from the clutch of men. So pretty! I could keep you, I should—oh, how I would! Too fine you are to rot in the world." She danced them through the currents. "But a treasure finer yet I will have—if I put you back. But, oh, it is hard!" She clutched at Sigurd. "Kiss me, pretty one! Oh, kiss me!"

Sigurd took her lips with his own. Her delicate hands flitted over his body, swirling him into a heady dream of lust and mystery.

The dream shattered suddenly with the press of cold, firm ground under his back. Her form above him was as light as a thought. The moon painted a slim hand as it flicked teasingly at his nose, and she laughed like a wild, fey thing, her lips parting over her sharp little teeth. Gold seemed to drip from her long, wet hair, and she laughed once more—then was gone with a splash.

"Sigurd!"

He lurched upright at Gunnar's call. He had forgotten Gunnar, had lost the thought of his friend in the thought of the mysterious female. But here Gunnar was, crouched on the riverbank, safe and inexplicably dry, as Sigurd was.

"Gunnar, did you …" Sigurd trailed off, looking out at the silvery surface of the water, unable to ask, unwilling to share. Gunnar turned, silent, to where their clothes and gear lay, these also dry when they should not be.

They dressed and gathered their things and stood to survey the shattered city. Moonlight washed the broken faces of buildings and spilled over the rubble that lay within crumbled streets, as though everything had been smashed with a gigantic club. Fine edges showed among the fragments, the stone expertly dressed and chiseled with elaborate patterns. Sigurd and Gunnar picked their way through it, clambering over the scattered stones, leaping across huge, crudely cut gouges.

As they drew near the cliff, the stone path showed more clearly. It led steeply to the wide, dark mouth. At the foot of the path, Sigurd and Gunnar looked at one another. Then Sigurd set his face and started up the slope. The path, though wide enough for a wagon, was treacherous with rubble and more of the deep gouges that had marked the city. In places, four would lie parallel, evenly spaced.

A wide porch lay at the top. Sigurd and Gunnar stood before the swath of darkness, staring into the mouth of the cliff. Remnants of carving surrounded the opening, though the opening itself was jagged, like part of it had been torn away, the mouth brutally widened. Deep within, firelight flickered.

With Gunnar at his heels, Sigurd crept into the dark cave, where a sulfurous reek choked them with every careful step among the rubble. As they drew nearer the fire, which burned in a massive hearth, it painted light over huge pillars of stone that stretched from floor to ceiling. The floor itself, though filthy and strewn with debris, was revealed to be smooth and even, patterned with blue and red. No cave, this, but the remains of a vast, fine hall. Outside the fire's circle, light was caught here and there, casting a glitter and shine through the darkness.

Sigurd felt a tug at his cloak and realized how near he had drawn to the light. He ducked behind a pillar and felt Gunnar close at his back, breathing against his neck. A white shape moved at the edge of the firelight, ghostly and familiar.

"What do you want, witch?" The voice rumbled from the darkness like a brewing storm.

Lofnheith drifted into the light in her tattered gown, her ashy hair drifting like tendrils of mist. "To see," she said. "To see."

A growl sounded, so low that Sigurd felt it more than heard it. Lofnheith stood with the fire at her back, facing the rumbling darkness. Something impossibly heavy dragged itself across the floor, punctuated by a four-beat clicking, and the firelight teased a curving gleam from the shadows. Then a set of four massive talons, each as tall as a man, drummed to the floor, sharp are scythes. High above, the light shone on the underside of a bearded, reptilian chin.

"And what is it that you want to see?" rumbled the dragon.

Chapter Nine

FIRE AND ASH and blood and gold."
    At Lofnheith's words, the dragon let out a gusty sigh that made her white gown stream like a tattered banner. The fire nearly blew out but licked and crackled and bloomed again. Fafnir settled into its light, snaking his long, spiked neck to the ground. His eyes gleamed small and bright, like dark jewels faceted to catch every color. Glistening, coppery scales started small at the end of his tapered snout and swept up to the crown of his horned head then along his neck, growing larger and darker until they disappeared into the shadows that hid his body. The scales ranged from red to gold, and they were rubbed pale and clean in places; in others they were streaked bluish-green with age and disuse.

"You exhaust me," grumbled the dragon.

"Fire-wyrm, gold-keeper, life-eater, hiding in the dark, a thread spun and suspended, waiting to be cut."

Fafnir's chin rose from the ground, the threads of his scaly beard quivering. "Cut? And who could cut *me*?"

"Live, he said, and thrice be burned and thrice be burned again," Lofnheith sang out. "Live, he said, and suffer—until the thread be cut, until your blood be in the deed, so I curse you. I remember now. I see it."

The hooked nostrils flared with a breath that billowed, sulfurous, through the hall. "You wake me from the bliss of golden sleep to speak your weird words?" The claws drummed on stone. "Should I not smite you?"

Lofnheith reached up a hand as though to touch the beast towering above. "Would that you could. Burn, he said, and live."

"Yes, well." Fafnir's head dropped to the ground. "That is your trouble, not mine."

Lofnheith's voice took on a rare, hard edge. "A god's death I saw in a clamp of gleaming teeth. Yours, I thought, noble and fierce, but fat you are with greed and malice, no different from the rest. More man than beast, whatever skin you wear."

Fafnir's tail, ridged with spikes, the end sharp as a whip's lash, snapped briefly into the light then slipped again into darkness. "What do you want, witch?"

"Blood and fire and bones burned black. A shower of shining gold."

Fafnir chuckled, a sound that rumbled through the floor. "And you call me malicious, sister."

"Dark my thoughts, and so alone." Lofnheith covered her face with her hands. "Are you even here? Is this now? Or before? Or after?"

"I am here, weird sister."

Lofnheith flung herself down beside the dragon's massive head, larger than her entire body. She stroked the shining scales of his face, caressed the prominent bones of his nose toward the short horns that grew back from the base of his skull. His nostrils and the bony ridges above his closed eyes were limned with light.

"You were always so beautiful like this, sweet monster," said Lofnheith, and Fafnir sighed.

The dragon, for all his horror, was indeed beautiful. Some deep part of Sigurd longed to touch him, to feel with his hands the impossible power. It seemed to not belong in this world. At Sigurd's back, Gunnar inhaled. It startled Sigurd, for he had entirely forgotten that Gunnar was there. He felt a question in Gunnar's breath. That breath meant, perhaps, We should go, but Sigurd had no intention of leaving, not yet.

The fire died, crumbling to embers, and the shadows seeped in until Sigurd could only imagine Lofnheith's crumpled form and Fafnir's great stillness.

Time suspended itself in the dark.

When it happened, it happened so quickly, the silence and darkness were shattered so completely, that it did not seem real, not at first. Gunnar shifted. So small was the movement, so quiet the whispering of his foot over the grimy floor that it barely stirred the air around them. But ... his foot disturbed something, and that something rolled and pinged, tiny and metallic, across the stones.

The dragon's massive bulk reared off the floor like a wave, and the fire that exploded from him sheared the air of the hall. Another blast arced high and wide. Flames caught here and there, on a decaying tapestry, on a broken door, in pools of shimmering oil, and the light was captured and cast everywhere by the gold and silver and the many-colored gems scattered and heaped in what had been the shadows of that great space.

The head of the dragon, snaking on a lithe and arching neck, reached nearly to the high, rough vault of the ceiling. Thick with age and old muscle, the body widened through the chest and belly, and sail-like wings fanned out angrily from behind his shoulders, shuddering. Under the scaled skin of his forelegs, huge ropes of muscle twisted and strained, clenching the bladed claws. Dense, powerful haunches and the deadly tail held him towering.

When Gunnar turned to run, the dragon crashed to the floor, cracking the stones and sending a tremor through the earth. He wound, serpent-like, through the hall and whipped around behind the boys. Sigurd yanked his sword from its scabbard to meet the huge face mere inches from his own. The dark, glittering eyes transfixed him, and the dragon's thin lips stretched into a grin. Yellowed teeth, thicker than Sigurd's legs, longer than his sword, jutted from the dark gums, and his sulfurous breath washed forth.

"Boy, you couldn't scratch my itch with that. Isn't he funny, sister?" Fafnir swung his head to look for Lofnheith, grunting to find that she had vanished.

Freed from the dragon's gaze, Sigurd leapt forward, his sword flashing toward the dark eye. Fafnir twitched at the movement and Sigurd missed the eye—but knocked loose a shining red scale below it. The dragon reared back, and a screeching roar tore through the air. Like a striking snake, he snapped at Sigurd, but Sigurd thrust up his sword. Fafnir caught it in his teeth and spat it out. The sword clattered away into the shadows.

Gunnar, who had stood like stone since the dragon circled them, stumbled back, tripping over a golden byrnie. Fafnir seized Gunnar in one clawed grip and Sigurd in the other, caging them with scaly fingers as thick as branches, and far stronger. Holding the boys aloft, Fafnir lumbered deeper into the hall, back to his shadowed hoard.

"Only thieves and cowards sneak about in the dark," said the dragon as he settled onto his haunches, his leathery wings folding noisily behind him. "Did you think to steal a coin? Perhaps a ring or a ruby or a golden cup?" Fafnir looked from one boy to the other with his terrible, dark eyes. "Speak!"

Gunnar flinched, but Sigurd said, "We are neither thieves nor cowards."

"Little heroes, then? Come to kill the dragon?" Fafnir gave a low, rumbling chuckle then looked to Gunnar. "Where is *your* weapon, little hero? Undrawn, I see. At least your friend tried." Fafnir's glittering eyes narrowed to thoughtful slits. Then he brought Gunnar close to his snout and sniffed. "You smell terribly familiar."

The dragon's thin lips curled back from jagged rows of teeth as he sneered. "You're a Nibelung. Disgusting. It took two hundred years to polish that smell out of my gold. Wait. Perhaps that's not it." Fafnir sniffed again, his hooked nostrils flaring. "Ah. My shriveled little brother—I certainly know *that* smell. Has he sent you for the hoard? He craves it most wickedly."

"Is that what you think?" called a voice from the entrance, where a dark shape blotted out a patch of the glittering stars.

"That I want the hoard? That is all you can think of, you murderous brute."

The dragon's eyes widened briefly then he pulled his face down into a cruel grin. "Regin. Are these yours?"

Regin stepped into the light of the scattered, flickering fires. His face was pale and grim above his dark clothes, and his eyes glinted like ice. "They are something to me. What are they to you?"

"Pesky little fleas, crawling among my things. And what does one do with fleas but crush them between two fingers?" Fafnir's grip tightened, eliciting grunts from both boys.

"Fingers? Do you still think yourself a man, brother? Look at yourself."

"*You* would scorn *my* form? You miserable, shrunken thing. How my father hated the sight of you."

"Don't pretend. He hated all of us. Only Otter did he value—and only once his pelt was solid gold and his guts were ropes of pearl. Then he loved that gilded carcass most fiercely."

"Do not speak of Otter that way!" Fafnir's tail whipped out and slapped the ground near Regin, nearly shaking him from his feet. The tail slipped back to the hoard and found the otter, frozen in gold, mouth yawning wide in a mockery of life. Fafnir's tail gently touched the treasure then slid away.

Regin said, "He is long dead, brother."

"And yet you covet him, like all the rest. And these." Fafnir shook the boys in his fists.

"Yes, I want those—and I will trade you for them."

Fafnir narrowed his jeweled eyes. "What could you possibly offer me?"

"This." Regin held up his right hand, where a gold ring gleamed on his forefinger.

Fafnir let out a shattering cry, and his claws sprang open. His captives fell to the hard floor, scrambling away as the dragon's forefeet crashed down, shaking the earth. Fafnir slithered across the hall to Regin, scattering treasure.

He coiled tight like a snake poised to strike and demanded, "How is it that *you* have the ring?"

Regin held the dragon's gaze. "I've always had the ring."

"Give it to me!"

"I said I would trade it."

"And why should I not rip the ring from your mangled corpse?"

The gold band vanished from Regin's hand, and he smiled his wolf-smile. "And how would you manage that?"

Fafnir growled, and the sound rumbled the floor, shifting treasure.

"I will trade it, as I said. For the boys."

"They mean that much to you?" Fafnir scoffed.

Without shifting his gaze from the dragon, Regin shouted, "Sigurd! Gunnar! Get over here."

Sigurd helped Gunnar to his feet, for Gunnar's leg had been hurt in the fall and could not bear his weight. Fafnir growled as they hurried through the hall, stumbling over treasure. His tail lashed, and smoke swirled from his nostrils, but his gaze was fixed on the ring.

"Out!" Regin commanded, and Sigurd supported Gunnar through the jagged archway.

Regin was framed in the entrance, the fire and the dragon before him, the ring held aloft, pinched now between his thumb and forefinger, gleaming. "Did you not know it was gone?"

"Of course I knew! Some trick of Loki's I thought it. I should have known you were just as cunning."

Regin gave a low laugh—and flung the ring deep into the hall. It pinged and rolled. With a shout like thunder, the dragon whipped away to chase it, his body a flash of red and gold and he snaked through the shadows. Regin rocked forward as though to chase the ring himself, then he wheeled away and grabbed each boy by the cloak.

⁂

The stunted forest to the east was a tangled net of warped limbs, but better their scraping branches and gnarled roots than the vast open stretch of the Heath—not that Fafnir would likely emerge. For generations he had lain quiet and cold among the silver and gold and glittering jewels. Now he had the ring to brood over as well. Regin rubbed at the bare spot on his finger and grimaced. He was naked without it, nothing.

The boys had not spoken, not as they fled down the rubble-strewn slope and through the ruins of the once-fine city, not as they came to Regin's hidden boat and took it across to the woods where he had left his horse and gear, not even as they began to travel south. Regin had said nothing either, for he could not trust his tongue, not right now. The ring. They had cost him *the ring*. A red haze clouded his vision, and his hands shook with violence until he had to stop and bend over his knees to still them.

"Regin, are you—"

Snarling, Regin struck Sigurd hard across the face. Gunnar, astride Regin's horse, made a sound of protest, but Sigurd only straightened, his cheek blooming red from the blow. Regin snarled again and walked on.

All day they walked, Gunnar dozing in the saddle and Sigurd trying not to stumble in his weariness. Gunnar asked Sigurd to ride, but he refused; the horse already bore Regin's gear and Gunnar's weight as well, for his ankle was swollen with sprain.

It was not until they camped that night that Regin relented enough to scold them. "Fools, both of you."

"It was a mistake," said Gunnar, shuddering, his face waxen in the firelight, like something that could melt. "A terrible mistake."

Sigurd frowned and jabbed a stick into the flames to move the logs and make them pop. Then he gazed across the fire to where Regin sat on the other side. "Will you tell us?"

Regin narrowed his icy eyes. "Tell you what?"

"The story."

Regin stared at Sigurd, marveling that he could be so simple, wondering if he really was. Why not ask first of the ring? Why not level an accusation of lying, of concealment at least? But the boy, cheek bruising blue, only waited for Regin to speak.

Regin said, "Tell me first why you went there."

"We followed Lofnheith," answered Gunnar, his eyes darting to Sigurd. "She is strange, and we were curious."

Regin raised a dark eyebrow. "Curious enough to step into a dragon's lair? A powerful curiosity, that."

"Why did she go to him?" asked Sigurd. "It seems not in her nature."

"What could you know of Lofnheith's nature? There is not a word, a look, a thought from her that you could trust."

"She speaks as though …"

"She sees the future?" Regin supplied when Sigurd trailed off. "Aye. And the past. And lives not her own. She is a thousand twisted threads, so tangled you could never follow one to the truth. She walks her own dark and twisted path, and whatever purpose she serves, it is not your good. I warned you once: she is dangerous."

All this Regin had long known to be true, yet when she had arrived at his house a year, to the very day, before Sigurd, he had opened his door to her, wanting those twisting words in spite of himself. Little good had it done him.

Sigurd gazed into the fire, clearly troubled. Regin wanted to snarl him into argument again.

"How is it," asked Gunnar, "that your brother … is so …"

"So *what*, Gunnar?" Regin pressed nastily.

Gunnar blanched then seemed to recover himself. His jaw firmed. "You have some explaining to do as well. Our actions might have been foolish—"

"The magnitude of your understatement astounds me."

"—but that does not change the fact that you have concealed much, even lied." Of course it was Gunnar, not Sigurd, who thought to address this point.

"None of it was yours to know, and it does not excuse your actions."

"Please, Regin," said Sigurd in his simple way, and something about it made Regin sigh and concede, "I suppose it is a tale I must now tell."

He had always intended to tell it but had wanted to choose his time, to frame it himself. More than that, he had expected to speak with the ring upon his finger, bolstered by its power and promise. Regin stared into the fire, brooding until he could master his tongue.

Then he began. "The ability to change form is common in the old blood. Giants and dwarves and elven kind once roamed more freely in this world. You may someday ask yourself why the gods saw fit to order all as they did, whom it served to so divide the worlds—which they so freely travel. Someday, indeed, you may wonder.

"My people were descended from those early races, and shape-changing was known to many. Fafnir learned to take his dragon form as a boy, but our other brother was different. Otter was so named because that was the shape in which he was born. Rarely did he appear as a man at all. He favored his sleek pelt and the waters of a deep pool that lay under a fall some distance up the river.

"One day as Otter lay on the bank of that pool eating a fish, it happened that Loki and Odin came traveling downriver toward the Rhine. When they came upon Otter, Loki took up a stone and threw it, striking Otter in the head and killing him."

"Three eyes upon the deed, though one hand threw the stone."

"What?" Regin demanded at Sigurd's murmured interruption.

"It was something Lofnheith said. I didn't understand it at the time."

Regin frowned. She had spoken much to the boy, mangled though her words had been. Why? What did she see?

"Please go on," said Sigurd. "Loki killed Otter and then …?"

"And *then* he cut the skin from Otter's body, gutted and quartered him. He did not know, or so he later claimed, that he had killed and mutilated the son of a king. All this came to light when Odin and Loki came to Hreidmar's hall seeking shelter for the night. From a bulging leather bag stained with blood, Loki pulled Otter's skin and held it up for the king to see. Even now, I recall how the light shone through the eyeholes, how terrible it was. Loki said, 'I killed this beast not an hour ago. The skin is a gift for you, king. Let us all feast on his sweet flesh.'

"Hreidmar let out a yell of such ferocity that the hall echoed with it. While he had not the gift of shape-changing, his blood held other magic. He snared the gods with words of binding and justice. So enraged was he that I feared he would kill Odin and Loki then and there. That would have brought the wrath of all the gods down upon us, so I spoke and said, 'Let them tell us how this has happened. Let us see then what is best to do.'"

Regin fingered the bridge of his nose. Still he remembered the crack of breaking bone as Hreidmar struck him for speaking in the hall, which he had been forbidden to do. Still he remembered the flow of blood and bitterness.

He left out that part and went on with the tale. "So Loki told of his mistake. He swore he had not known Otter was anything but a simple beast and swore to pay the most astonishing wergild ever known. He would sew together the otter skin to give it form again. He would fill it with gold and other treasures. Hreidmar said Loki must gild the outside as well, leaving not one hair uncovered. Loki agreed.

"How he acquired the wergild I know only by Loki's own account, given upon his return. When he left Hreidmar's kingdom, he traveled first to the sea goddess Nan and borrowed from her—stole, more likely—a net that could capture any water creature. With the net he returned to the pool where he had killed Otter. None of us knew this until Loki told his story, but another creature, in the shape of a pike, also dwelled under the fall. But Andvari's other form was not that of a man, for Andvari was a dwarf.

"Andvari had in his possession the entire wealth of his people, and when Loki caught him with the magical net, he forced Andvari to dive again and again into the water to bring up the gold and jewels." Sigurd's eyes flew to Gunnar, whose face had turned hard and cold as iron. Regin, lost in his story, did not notice. "Loki gilded the outside of the otter skin and began to stuff the treasure through the mouth. But no matter how much he stuffed into the skin, it never seemed to fill. Hreidmar's trickery, of course. Not until every bit of the treasure had been taken was the skin full at last. Then Loki returned with it and Hreidmar was appeased."

A few things Regin left out. The ring that Andvari had tried to hold back but which Loki had seen glinting in the water. And the curse, of course, that Andvari had laid upon the treasure when Loki demanded that final piece. Also this: how Loki had tried to keep the ring for himself, yielding it only when Hreidmar pointed out an uncovered whisker. Then there had been Hriedmar's obsession with the hoard, the way he would sit in the treasury weighing it in his hands, counting the pieces, obsessed.

Regin skipped ahead to Fafnir's crime. "Fafnir craved that treasure something terrible, and one day he drew his sword and thrust it into Hriedmar's back, spilling his father's blood amid the gold and jewels. Ever since has he held the hoard, adding much to it, for none lust for blood and gold like a dragon."

The rest of the story—Fafnir's madness after the murder, his massacre of the people in the hall, his destruction of the city and surrounding countryside—Regin did not tell. He said nothing of how Fafnir had cast him out, forcing him into the world of men and servile work. He spoke not a word of the ring he had pulled from Hreidmar's cooling finger while Fafnir raged, the ring that been the balm to his pride, the bite in his words, the promise of his revenge.

He would get the ring back—and more besides.

On the evening of their return, Sigurd's gaze flew to the roof of Regin's house. Lofnheith's birds were gone. Mad she might have been, and perhaps she had betrayed them into danger, yet he was saddened to think he might not see her again. Perhaps now he would better understand her words. Perhaps she could tell him more of the dragon, for Regin's story had skimmed past so much.

Gazing now at the roof peak, Sigurd noticed something he had not before. The strangely twisted carving, which he had long dismissed as meaningless, took on a clear shape. The curled top was a looped, spiked tail, and twisting down from it was the warped and broken body of a dragon. *There is one man I hate above all.* Regin's words, spoken a year ago on the journey from Denmark. It was Fafnir he had meant, the man who had killed his own father—the man who was the dragon.

Unreal it seemed, that terrible power and beauty, in the light of day, in the quiet river valley, approaching the simple wattle fence of Regin's yard. Besides, something more pressing demanded Sigurd's attention, for a cluster of riders milled about within. Gunnar cried, "Hogni!"

A richly dressed boy of perhaps thirteen winters broke away from the group of men. "Gunnar!"

Passing through the gate, Gunnar swung down from Regin's horse, landing on his good leg, and limped over to his brother, putting off the question of what pained him to get at once to the reason Hogni was there.

The younger boy, his hair the same dark shade as Gunnar's but his face and body thinner, clasped Gunnar fiercely then leaned back to say, "Father calls for you. There is war."

"Who?"

Hogni grimaced. "Atli. King Budli died last month. Poison, some say. Atli is now king."

Gunnar's mouth twisted. "And he attacks, with his father's ashes yet on the wind. That snake."

Hogni gripped Gunnar's arm. "Brother, come home."

"Of course," said Gunnar. "Of course I will come. There is nothing for me here anyway."

Something in Sigurd dimmed at those words. Whatever friendship he and Gunnar had built, it would be nothing now that Gunnar's brother was here. In an instant, he saw this. In an instant, too, he realized that he did not want to be alone again. But then Gunnar looked to Regin and said, "You will release my foster brother to come with me."

Regin smiled a small, secret smile. "Of course he must go with you."

Gunnar turned to Sigurd, and a hint of uncertainty entered his eyes. "Sigurd? Will you fight with me? I would not have you stay here."

Clasping Gunnar's offered forearm, Sigurd grinned. "I would not have you go alone. But," he added with a pang, "I have lost my sword."

Gunnar's grip on Sigurd's arm tightened in solidarity. "We will find you one."

The house was silent with the boys gone, with Lofnheith gone, with even the owl gone. Regin was surprised to feel lonely as he sat at the hearth, idly prodding the fire. The crackle and pop of wood did little to fill the space, but the loneliness would pass, as it always did. Regin knew how to wait. He knew, too, that this was necessary, reminded himself that it was the very reason he had laid poison into that letter he had sent to King Budli with the commissioned sword—for how should a boy become a man mighty enough to face a dragon if he did not wade first through the weeds of war?

About the Author

Katherine Buel is a fantasy novelist and avid horsewoman. She has an MFA from Northern Michigan University and has lived in eight different states.

Manufactured by Amazon.ca
Bolton, ON